ALSO BY JANE LOUISE CURRY

The Ice Ghosts Mystery
The Lost Farm
Parsley Sage, Rosemary and Time
The Watchers
The Magical Cupboard

(MARGARET K. MC ELDERRY BOOKS)

POOR TOM'S
GHOST

POOR TOM'S GHOST

Jane Louise Curry

A Margaret K. McElderry Book

ATHENEUM 1977 NEW YORK

Floor plan and drawings by the author

Calligraphy by Philip Bouwsma

Library of Congress Cataloging in Publication Data
Curry, Jane Louise. Poor Tom's ghost.
"A Margaret K. McElderry book."
Summary: When they inherit a house built in
1603, a contemporary London family is drawn into
a real Shakespearian tragedy.
[1. Space and time—Fiction. 2. London—
Fiction] I. Title.
PZ7.C936Po [Fic] 76-28468
ISBN 0-689-50072-6

Published simultaneously in Canada by
McCelland & Stewart, Ltd.
Manufactured in the United States of America by
Halliday Lithograph Corporation
West Hanover, Massachusetts
Designed by Suzanne Haldane
First Edition

FOR JUDY DUNBAR
. . . day is day, night, night, and time is time

Poor Tom

He puts on Hell like a suit of clothes
To wear it walking in the Town,
For who would think that Hell could pose
As a London suit and French silk hose
Out buying its lady a satin gown
Or giving a beggar half a crown?

Poor Tom

It strolls on aimless, well-shod feet
To buy its wine and cheese and bread.
It smiles at maidens roundly sweet
And helps blind crones across the street.
It moves its eyes and turns its head,
For it's alive and poor Tom's dead.

Poor Tom

—OLD SONG

POOR TOM'S GHOST

Fie on't, ah fie, tis an unweeded garden

HAT ARE WE LOOKING FOR?" ROGER
asked his father.

"A turning on the right." Tony slowed the old Ford estate car down to twenty and cast an uneasy eye at the boat trailer looming in the wing mirror. From time to time along Park Road a grey mini had drifted out so that its driver could peer around the dinghy on the trailer. He could not tell whether it meant to pass them or not. "It's along here somewhere—before the first house, according to Aunt Deb's Mr. Carey."

Jo, beside him, pointed. "Could that be it? Or is it just a break in the fence? It looks a bit jungly for a driveway."

Tony's eyebrows shot above his sunglasses as he

3

switched on the boat trailer's right-turn indicator and braked carefully to a crawl. "Unh! Knee-deep in grass. But if that's not it, I don't know what is. Roger?" He turned toward the back seat, the high spirits he had been in all the way from central London out to Isleworth a shade dimmed. "Be a good fellow and have a look out your window: If that nervous mini's still behind us, wave him round, and then nip across to see if that's the lane we want. I'm no good at backing this rig, so once we're in, we're in."

"O.K., Pa." Roger thrust his head out the rear window on the traffic side, saw the mini lurking and, after a quick look for oncoming traffic, beckoned violently. The little grey car and its plump, grey-haired driver swung out and past with a wave, slowing as it came abreast of the high brick wall ahead and turning left into Syon Park. Tony brought the Ford to a full stop, and ten-year-old Pippa caught hold of Sammy, the longtailed bushbaby, as Roger opened the car door.

Roger, gaining the opposite side of the tree-lined road and the grassy, gravelled track Jo had spotted, fought the urge to hunch over to ease the nervous spasm that tightened his stomach. Until just now it had not occurred to him that the house might be dreadful. A gingerbreaded monstrosity. A mildewed horror mouldering away under a mat of ivy. It might be anything. "A great house. Wait and see. You'll be mad about it," his father had said with an air of mystery. But if his dad hadn't seen it since he was a kid.... And actually, he had probably forgotten all about it until last week. Certainly he had never mentioned it during Roger's thirteen years. According to Great-aunt Deb's lawyer, it had been standing empty for

4

three months. That explained the overgrown drive, but what if it also meant mildew and damp rot, rising damp and woodworm, vandalism even, or vermin? It *couldn't*. Everything had been going so well all day. In fact, everything had been going so well since Friday a week ago when Tony gave his first performance in *Hamlet* at the National Theatre and earned himself a sheaf of favourable newspaper reviews. It couldn't fall apart now. They had sung the whole of the way down—"I'm Henery the Eighth, I Am!" and "If it Wasn't for the 'Ouses in Between." Even a tearjerking rendition of "If Those Lips Could Only Speak" in harmony.

The cramp in Roger's stomach bit sharply, but eased as he bent over to examine something in the grass beside a fencepost. Please God, he prayed fiercely, don't let Pa just take one look at it and dig in his heels.

Straightening, Roger yelled across the road. "Pa? This has to be it. There's a stone marker here with cox carved on it."

Tony acknowledged the news with a half-salute and after a television repair van coming from the direction of the river had passed, he pulled across the road in a neat arc, easing the single-axle trailer into the narrow lane with inches to spare.

"I do believe the old man's improving," quipped Roger as he climbed back in beside Pippa.

Jo gave a little snort of laughter, but Pippa looked at Roger solemnly, as if she sensed the tension under the flippant tone.

Tony pulled a long face. "Don't remind me. I'll have to repaint the gate at home after this afternoon's performance."

The lane, a right-of-way that did not actually belong to the old Cox property, ran narrowly between a brick wall on the left and the stout rail fence of the field to the right. Tony drove cautiously, with an eye on the right-hand wing mirror. Roger leaned back with one arm on the wicker cat carrier, trying to look unconcerned, but Pippa hung over the back of the front seat, watching eagerly for the first glimpse of a house.

Tony looked every bit as eager as Pippa, but Roger detected—or imagined that he did—a hint of defensive irony in his father's tone as he remarked, "Aunt Deb used to call it Castle Cox."

"Then we'll have to call it Castle Nicholas," Pippa said.

"Right you are, Pips."

Jo smiled lazily. "Tony, you're a fraud. You groan at the thought of being tied to a house, but you're as excited as a kid. You've never actually been *in* it, have you?"

Tony, driving with one hand, drummed his fingers rhythmically on the edge of the car roof. "Not much further in than the front door, but I thought it was a great place, what I saw of it. The old lady who lived here —she was my great-grandmother—" he explained to Pippa, "was ninety-three, and I was six or seven. Aunt Deb brought me down because she thought the old lady, hermit or no, might like to meet the last of the line before she shuffled off this mortal coil. An ancient female left us for what seemed hours in a long, high entrance hall full of dusty aspidistras, and in the end the old lady refused to see us at all. She'd quarreled with all of her relatives fifty years or more before and wasn't about to make it up. *Uh*-oh!" Tony braked quickly, then opened his door to lean out and look behind. Closing it resignedly, he said,

"Snagged again. Take a look, will you, Rog? What'll happen if I just keep on going?"

Roger clambered out to inspect the fencepost that had caught the trailer's right-hand mudguard. "You'd make it two in one day."

"Hell," Tony muttered. But he backed up several feet and then eased the trailer wheel safely past. "I was trying to keep well clear of the wall for the sake of our nice, fresh varnish," he grumbled, exaggerating blandly. The boat was not so wide as all that. "We shall just have to creep."

"Finish your story," Jo prompted. "If Great-grandmother Cox was ninety-three then, how old was she when she died?"

"Ninety-nine, the poor old witch. Only a hair short of a hundred. She missed her letter of congratulation from the Queen by three days. Then the house came to Aunt Deb as next-of-kin, and she wrote to me at school about it. It was crammed to the rafters with rubbish—newspapers, magazines, empty jars and tins—and every Christmas gift Aunt Deb had sent her for thirty years, every one of them still in its Christmas wrappings."

"But that's *crazy*," Pippa protested, wide-eyed. How could *anyone* not open a Christmas present?

"Crazy or nasty," Jo agreed, equally impressed.

Roger, who had never heard the tale of old Mrs. Cox before, forgot his careful pose of detached interest. "But Pa? If the house was left to Great-aunt Deb all that long ago, how come you never came back?"

"Oh, the place was too big for Aunt Deb, and too far from town, so she had it cleaned up and then let it. According to Mr. Carey, there was a steady stream of tenants up until the early sixties when a local builder took it over as a warehouse of sorts. He cleared out in '75, and since then the Children of Nod, one of Aunt Deb's obscure charities, have had it as a hostel."

"The Children of *Nod*? That's a funny name," Pippa said.

"It's from the Bible, isn't it?" asked Jo. " 'The land of Nod on the east of Eden' where Cain went after God cursed him for killing his brother Abel?"

Tony nodded. "Though I believe that the hostel took in rather less spectacular outcasts." He smiled. "Dear Aunt Deb. I wish she'd lived long enough to have been in the best seat in the stalls last Friday night to see my Hamlet. She was passionately fond of Shakespeare even if she did tend to muddle one play up with another. She always said I'd have my chance at Hamlet." He paused, frowning at the way ahead. "What have we here?"

Coming from the shade of the lane into a patch of bright August sunshine, the car's pace slowed from a creep to a full stop. The brick wall bent sharply to the left; the fence angled away to the right, and the grass-grown drive went both ways, disappearing into a jungly green shade.

" 'Fie on't, ah fie, 'tis an unweeded garden,' " Tony quoted—a shade apprehensively, Roger thought. And it was pretty bad. A machete and chain-saw would be more to the point in such a garden than Jo's nippers and clippers.

"Away with your pishery-pashery. It's a challenge!" Jo did an eeny-meeny between the two lanes and said decidedly, "Me for the right-hand way."

"Me too," Pippa seconded.

"Roger?"

"Me? Oh, whichever."

"Six of one and half a dozen of the other so far as I can see," Tony observed, taking the way on his right hand. "I don't actually remember, but I would guess that the driveway circles past the front of the house and back out again. For making sweeping entrances. I—" He broke off, stalling the car as he braked abruptly without engaging the clutch.

"Lawks-a-mussy!" Jo said inelegantly. She stared at the house that had materialized amidst the trees. "Tony, no! Tell me we've come wrong. We *have* come wrong, haven't we?"

For the house was awful. It was an ugly, streaked, once-pink pile, not so much large as lumpish: a tall, awkward box pretending to be a castle. The roof was bordered with a crumbling crenellated parapet and absurd little turrets strung like birthday candles along its length. The ground-floor windows were boarded up with plywood, the entrance porch and padlocked front door with corrugated metal sheeting.

"Goddlemighty, what a horror!" Tony shook his head unbelievingly. "I don't remember its being like this. Oh, *blast*! Can't you just hear what old Alan will have to say when he comes down on Sunday? Well, I won't have it. I won't be caught *dead* in that thing. It's so silly it's obscene—worse than that incredible Californian 'Royal Camelot Fish and Chip Palace' in Santa Monica."

"Castle Nicholas," Jo gasped. She tried hard not to laugh.

"Oh, shut up." Tony glowered.

Pippa, already struck silent, stroked Sammy and frowned at the house as if it were upside-down or out-of-focus, and squinting might help.

"Well," Tony said at last, "the first thing I do when we

9

get home tonight is telephone Alan and put him off for Sunday. If that idiot caught sight of this we'd be done for. 'Where's your sense of bloody humour?'" he mimicked. "'It could be the poor man's Strawberry Hill. Think of the hysterical parties you could throw.' No thanks."

"But we *can't* go home tonight!" Roger was stricken. "We brought the camp beds and sleeping bags. And the boat. What about the boat? You said we could take it out on the river tomorrow or Sunday. We've not had it out in two years." He opened his door and jumped out, his mind racing like a squirrel in a cage. The house was beyond apology, but..."Even if we don't stay, we should leave the boat here if there's a garage. 'No more than a thousand feet from the river'—isn't that what that solicitor, Mr. Carey said?"

"Um." Tony moodily rested his chin on his wrists crossed on the steering wheel. "I suppose we ought to. August isn't the month to look for a mooring on the Thames. And I did promise. Jo?"

"Who, me? Please yourself. I can stand anything for a weekend so long as there aren't bats. One bat and I'm on my way back to Hamilton Terrace."

"Helpful, aren't you? Well then, we'll see..."

Roger was off and away. "I'll see if there is a garage," he called over his shoulder. Behind him, Jo was already out of the car, stretching her elegant, skinny length, and a martyred Tony was re-starting the motor so that he could pull up in front of the house. Oh pleasissimus, God, thought Roger, let us stay the weekend and Alan come Sunday and make Pa see the house could be a wonderful joke. And make Alan bring Jemmy so he can't flirt with

Jo and sink Pa in the sulks. We may never again have a chance at a house.

Not that the Nicholases were precisely hard up. Tony was a successful actor and besides his fairly steady stage work in London, had over the past ten years made good money in films. But there was precious little to show for it. Tony was sentimental, generous, occasionally bloody-minded, occasionally melancholy, usually cheerful, and incapable of saving tenpence. If he decided to sell the house Great-aunt Deb had left him before they found another that really suited, that would be the end of it. A few friends with hard-luck stories, a few splashy parties, perhaps a new and bigger sailboat—on top of a whacking tax bill from the Inland Revenue—and farewell house-money.

If the Nicholases *had* ever felt a pinch, Tony and Jo might have grown a shade uneasy with their butterfly existence. But somehow there was always good food, a comfortable flat, even a garden for Pippa's pets and Jo's collection of potted herbs and flowers. That it was always somebody else's flat and garden never seemed to bother them. Their present perch in Hamilton Terrace in St. John's Wood was the sixth since their return the previous summer from a year in California. Jo had gone directly into rehearsals for a play at the Lyric, and Tony had the good luck to be invited to rejoin the National Theatre Company shortly after its move to the new complex on the Thames' Bankside. Neither had time to spare for house-hunting. And, after all, why rent when the Overburys were off to New York for a two-month stint in a play there and had offered the use of their house off Chelsea Green? Muswell Hill, Farm Place, Oak Village, Campden Hill and Hamilton Terrace had followed, each offer turning up as if on cue. The world was full of friends.

After all they were charming, the Nicholases, footloose and amusing. Everyone said so. "Of course Pippa is a bit of a puzzle, but wonderfully decorative, my dear, with that cloud of red-gold hair and that sweet wide-eyed animal—what is it? a bushbaby?—always on her shoulder. And Roger? Quite the charmer. Another five years and Tony will have to look to his laurels. Wonderful family. Weathered some rough seas, too."

Wonderful, maybe. So everyone said. But seaworthy? More like a four-log raft lashed together with string and sticking plaster. Having a house of their own might not change anything, but. . . . Roger, rounding the east corner of Castle Cox, drew a deep breath and shut his eyes thankfully. There was a garage: an ugly cement-block box of a thing with corrugated iron doors, but a garage.

"Found it, Pa!" Roger called.

Tony appeared with his hands in his jeans pockets and a faintly mulish curve to his mouth. "The question is, is it long enough?"

"Plenty long. Look." Roger disappeared into the thick shrubbery alongside the garage. "It runs back this way a good twenty feet. The boat's only fourteen."

When he reappeared, Tony had produced the ring of keys provided by Mr. Carey and was trying one in the padlock. "There you go." The hinges screeched as together they opened the leaves of the door wide on a long, bare shelter roofed with corrugated green plastic panels. "A poor thing, but our own," Tony quipped sourly. "I reckon the simplest course will be to pull round here to unhitch, and then run the trailer in by hand. If we decide not to stay, we can still go by the river and have a look at the slipway before we head home."

"It's already four o'clock," Roger said nervously as they headed back to the car. "If we do have to go, shouldn't we wait until the worst of the traffic's over?"

"On a Friday it's the outbound traffic that's bad. It shouldn't be too heavy going in, even—" Tony broke off. "Here Pippa! We don't want all that gear off-loaded. I said we'd *see*."

Roger grinned. While Jo poked around in the shrubbery —looking for what, he could not guess—Pippa had calmly begun piling bundled camp beds, sleeping bags, carryalls, lawn chairs and the smaller of the cartons of groceries in a heap beside the wide doorstep in front of the armour-clad entryway at the corner of Castle Cox. Sammy's carrier and Spencer-the-snake's gallon glass jar stood side by side on the step.

"I'm sorry." Pippa did not look particularly apologetic, though. " 'We'll see' always ends up 'Oh, all right,' so I thought I'd save time."

Tony contemplated her with raised eyebrows. "Fox! Still, I suppose 'We'll see' *is* playing for time in the face of defeat. You're quite right."

"About what?" Jo drifted up, waving a dry palm frond. "Looky. We have a midget palm tree on the far side of the jungle."

"About staying the weekend. All the world's little shuffles are transparent as glass to your daughter." Tony tossed her the key ring. "Do the honours, will you? I'll root out the ruddy tire iron to use on those window boards."

But when he went to open the car's trunk, he was hum-

13

ming *"Any old iron, any old iron ... Any, any, old, old iron?"* and Roger knew things were looking up.

The oddest thing about the Nicholas family, as Roger saw it, was that they were one at all. His life, and his father's, had been so haphazard for so long that even though more than two years had passed since Tony and Jo were married, it seemed incredible that their luck could still hold.

Tony, as an actor, was inclined to spend more time and attention getting himself inside other people's skins than paying much attention to those details of everyday life other parents worried over: regular bedtimes, school, meals, and clean socks and underclothing. Roger's own mother had died when he was three, and Tony, in his distraction, had deposited him in Ealing with Granny Nicholas and headed back to Nottingham's repertory company to plunge himself into work. Two years later, having made something of a name for himself at Nottingham and in an Oxford Playhouse production of a Stoppard play, he had as suddenly reappeared. But after three years in London with the National Theatre Company at the Old Vic—lived half in Ealing and half who-knows-where—he left again, this time to join the Royal Shakespeare Company at Stratford. When Granny died, he had simply added Roger to the luggage he took on tour to America, Australia, and back.

For an older child it might have been an interesting life, easygoing and hectic at the same time; but it was precarious, too. There were missed meals, erratic schooling, too many strange hotel rooms and, at home in London (wherever home might be at the moment), long evenings alone with homework and the television set. All

14

that, mixed with being fussed over, resented, or ignored by Tony's successive girl friends, had left him at the age of eleven with his father's disarming grin and curly dark hair, a nervous stomach, and a humourous, gregarious manner that masked the daily dread that everything was going to fall apart: that now his father was well known, making good money, endlessly busy, Roger would be packed off to boarding school and forgotten.

Jo Parkin had appeared out of the blue: auburn-haired, American, divorced, and Pippa's mother, playing opposite Tony in a televised version of *Women Beware Women*. They had worked together years before without paying much attention to each other. This time round, they had a hard time paying attention to the play. Jo was, if it were not a contradiction in terms, a glamorous old shoe—generous, quirky, unflappable. Pippa was a quieter, shyer version of the same.

They were not long in making up their minds. They were married between rehearsals for Shaw's *On the Rocks*, and though life went on as erratically as before, it seemed at first to Roger as if it had against all reason righted itself—as if he might not be in danger of falling overboard after all. But since the spring the four of them seemed to have drifted further and further apart. With Jo up before dawn and off to the film studio until just last week, and Tony caught up in preparations for taking over the role of Hamlet for two months, there were days when "family" came down to Roger and Pippa sharing scrambled-egg sandwiches in front of the television.

So Roger, when Great-aunt Deb died and left Tony a house, had fastened onto it as the only answer. With all the Nicholases' comings and goings, what they needed was a safe harbour.

15

Whofe there?

HE TIRE IRON, AS IT HAPPENED, WAS unnecessary. Once indoors, Tony found that the boarding was secured by hooks that were easily reached when the lower window sashes were raised halfway, and the upper ones lowered. To his surprise, several of the hooks were rusted in place.

"Odd. These couldn't have rusted fast so quickly," he muttered, straining to loosen a stubborn one. "You'd think they'd been in place since the time the house was used as a warehouse. Do you suppose the Children of Nod were all in Aunt Deb's head?"

Jo sniffed tentatively. "No, I detect an aroma of mouse

and man. It's not been empty long or you'd smell the dreadful decay."

She flicked the light-switch hopefully, but with the electricity off, predictably, nothing happened. However, with the large room off the hallway opened up, there was light enough in the ground-floor rooms to give even Roger pause. While Pippa explored, he stood rooted in dismay in the wide doorway between the entrance hall and the room that must once have been a sitting-room or parlour, clutching the camp-stove to his chest as if it were an over-sized talisman against despair.

The hall was not only not "long and high" as Tony had remembered it, but was dreadful to boot. It ran the length of the northeast side of the house and up a flight of stairs to a landing dimly lit by a stained-glass window in muddy purples and browns. The entire length was papered down to a waist-high moulding in a dirty grey-and-pink pattern like a flecked linoleum, and every twelve or so inches a deformed pink and yellow duck soared off in the direction of the landing window. Below the strip-moulding the wall was covered with a heavy embossed paper last painted a glossy black. Where the wallpaper above was blotched brown with age, the lower was buckled and furred at the bottom with dust. The dim expanse of ducks and dust was broken only by a single window and the doorway opposite.

The front room itself, though oddly proportioned, was not unpleasantly so. But little more could be said for it. Here and there paper sagged from the ceiling and walls in ragged festoons and the oak parquet was deeply scarred, as if the builder-tenant had shifted heavy equipment in and out with no care at all for the once-handsome floor. All that was left of the Children of Nod was a heap

17

of mouse-eaten mattresses tumbled into one corner of a smaller front room opening off the first, and a miscellany of rubbish in another corner: soiled, discarded clothing, boots without mates, frames without pictures, bundles of leaflets announcing that The End is Nigh, and a motor-way sign that read BRISTOL—*8 miles*.

"Do you know, I think they must have left these windows boarded up and lived in the dark," Tony said incredulously. "Or by electric light. A *most* peculiar lot, Aunt Deb's little charity. She can't have had Carey check them out or come down to see for herself."

"I suppose we must be thankful that it wasn't a hostel for homeless dogs or cats." Jo, edging past Roger with a sleeping bag under each arm, laughed as she caught the strained look on Roger's face. "For heaven's sake, you great lummox! We don't have to *leave* it this way. Not even for the weekend. A good airing and a good scrub will work wonders."

"It'll take more than that," Tony said as he moved into the next room. "It's too hot for a bonfire now, but tonight we'll burn every scrap that isn't nailed down: mattresses, rubbish, wallpaper, the lot."

"Lovely!" Jo dropped the sleeping bags in a corner and stretched like an elegant, bony cat. "I adore ripping wall-paper. The very word is luxurious. R-r-r-*rip*!"

" 'What depths of pure destruction a woman's smiles do paper o'er,' " Tony murmured, coming to the doorway of the shadowed rear room. His voice sounded strange as he said it, and Roger half imagined that he saw a bewildered look of pain flicker in his father's eyes.

It was gone in a moment if it had been there, and Tony went back to wrestling cheerfully with the bar-locks to the back room's French doors. Jo stood for a moment quite still, faintly perplexed, off balance, and Roger looked away quickly, not wanting to see in a hurt look that Tony had been needling her. He put the stove down and headed back for the hall.

Jo's voice followed him out. "We might as well chuck everything in the front room until we get straightened out."

"Whatever you say," Tony answered vaguely.

Pippa clattered down from upstairs and followed the fleeing Roger into the sun-dappled drive. "Rog? Will you carry Bast's thingummy? He's got too heavy for me." She bent over to unlatch the door to Sammy's carrier and coax out the curled-up bushbaby. In a moment he was on her shoulder, eyes screwed shut in fright and dislike of the sunlight's glitter. His tiny hands twined tightly in her fly-away hair.

"Sure." Roger reached into the car's back seat for the big cat basket. "Where do you want him?"

"Around in the back garden, I guess. Ow!" She winced as Sammy scrambled round to her other shoulder and grabbed at her earlobe to steady himself. "It's all right," she said quickly. "It was being left in the basket. He's never stopped being afraid we'd go off and leave him in quarantine again."

"We should have left him in California," Roger pointed out. "Then he wouldn't have had six months in a cage and all this to-ing and fro-ing."

"Ye-es. But then he wouldn't have me," Pippa returned unarguably. "And I think he'd *rather* have me."

"I suppose so." Roger was doubtful, but amused.

In the overgrown back garden Pippa headed for the

shade of a broad-limbed old horse-chestnut. While Roger fumbled with the fastener on Bast's door, she fished in her pockets and came up with a handful of dry cat crunchies to be shared between Bast and Sammy. Then she unscrewed the lid on Spencer-the-grass-snake's jar and reached in to stroke a finger down his silky spine.

She frowned as she replaced the perforated lid. "He's all excited. If I turn him loose now he might take off for good, so I think I'll wait. He'll like it here once he's not too hysterical to hang around."

"How can you tell he's excited?" Roger was genuinely curious. His small step-sister had been known to carry on long, incomprehensible conversations with birds and squirrels, and on one eerie afternoon in the London Zoo had talked for a good five minutes through a fence with a bewildered but fascinated wolf. It had been eerie because Roger could have sworn that they understood each other's growls and yips and snuffles. But—a snake? Spencer, so far as Roger had noticed, was not given to cocking his head or snuffling.

"Oh, that's easy." Pippa reached back to stroke Sammy. "You feel it through your fingers. A ripple like a pulse, almost. Besides, his head moves more, and his tongue flickers further out." She looked around for a clear spot at the edge of shade and sun. "He'll feel better when he's warmed up and had a drink."

Roger believed it. He had a sudden, almost overwhelming, urge to wrap his arms around Pippa in a bear hug and squeeze, the way she squeezed old Bast. But then Bast, when hugged, just hung there like a furry sack of flour, with a look of martyred boredom. Pippa not only might hug back, but she might begin to think that he needed looking after too. It was safer to enjoy her with the old detached amusement. She might be only ten to his thirteen, but the way she trotted around tidying up her universe and making all its creatures comfortable was— at a distance—somehow reassuring.

Or usually was. The garden's peace was suddenly shattered by an eldritch yowl as Bast burst through his basket's door and streaked for the open French doors where Tony struggled to shift an unwieldy plywood panel over the rail of the garden stairs. A shriek followed close upon the yowl.

"Mice! Three or four of them," Jo, hiccuping with laughter, called from the front room as Tony and the children came running. She held a slice of half-buttered bread and a buttery knife. "There *were* three or four, but fat old Bast chased them into the hall and straight out the front door. I hope he routs the whole population before nightfall. I don't much fancy waking tomorrow to a row of little corpses lined up like love gifts at the foot of my sleeping bag."

Roger grinned. "I wouldn't have thought he still had it in him."

"He did look more like a flying fur cushion than your usual mouser. Anyway, you're in, so come have your tea. The kettle won't be a moment."

It was already humming on the camp stove set up by an open window in the big front room, and a battered tea case had been rescued from the rubbish in another room, upended, and given a newspaper tablecloth. Crowded onto it were the bread on its cutting board, a large lump of cheese, a pint of milk, butter, and a slightly squashed chocolate cream cake. On the floor, a tin of biscuits, a pot of strawberry preserves, a mug full of cutlery, plates, and the teapot were set out on last Sunday's *Observer*.

"Hah! All the comforts of," Tony said ironically. But he took a piece of bread and butter and a large dollop of jam on a tin plate and, dusting off a seat on the steps between the front room and the rear one opening onto the garden, looked around him speculatively.

"I suppose it's not *quite* so bad from the inside. The proportions are almost all wrong, of course, but with a few changes it might just be possible. I wonder what possessed the late tenants to rip out the kitchen fittings." He nodded toward the smaller room off the front room. "It looks as if it must have been some time ago—there's no trace of water pipes or gas connections."

Jo smiled placidly. "Kitchen's down in the basement. The door and the stairs down to it are between the built-in cupboards and the far wall in the room behind you. And there's actually running water, which is a blessing."

"It may seem less a blessing when the bill comes," Tony said sourly. "I suspect it means that the Children of Nod have gone off without settling their account with the Water Board." He looked over his shoulder as he reached for the mug of tea Jo held out. "The room at the back would be the dining room, then. Perhaps the little one was a library. I *thought* it queer the only kitchenish room should be off such a front-parlourish one. It's still a bit peculiar, though. This doesn't really strike one as the sort of place to have a town-housey basement kitchen, does it?" His eyes narrowed with the expression of a man beginning to be caught up in a crossword puzzle. "I think I'll have a look round upstairs before we run the boat under cover, Roger. Parcel out the bedrooms."

"Fine with me," Roger said casually, struggling to mask his pleasure.

And then Pippa had to go and ruin it all.

"But what about all the holes in the roof up there?" she said.

At eleven Roger was still awake, kneeling in his briefs by the window of the bedroom he had chosen—in spite of the hole in the ceiling. But he was lost to the rising breeze, the laughter and closing-time murmur floating up from the riverside pub, the London Apprentice, and the insects' song woven through the leaves and grass like a net to cradle the sleeping house until morning. For Roger knelt there in a familiar dream, leaning out the window of a room all his own—a green and brown lair, book-strewn, music-filled, with a specially made case on one wall for his swimming trophies and on the far wall his double-poster-size blowup of the funny old photograph of Tony and Jo as Benedict and Beatrice in *Much Ado About Nothing*. It was a room so real that had Roger turned just then he would have been bewildered, frightened even, to see it shadow-filled, its walls and floors badly splotched with damp, and nothing in it but an old Safari camp bed.

It had been a good day, all in all. To judge from the damage already done to plaster ceilings and the panelled facing of the master bedroom and dining-room fireplaces, the holes in the roof were of long standing even though they were small enough to take no more than a day or two's repairing. *Not*, according to Tony, to be done by the lot who had gouged the good parquet floor into splinters. He had got a line on a roof-repair firm in Twickenham Road over a pint of bitters at the pub while Roger leaned happily on a fencepost above the slipway to watch the mud slopes disappear as the river broadened with the rising tide.

The little stretch of Church Street along the Thames from the London Apprentice to Ferry House and the Syon Park boundary wall had been a pleasant surprise: an open stretch along the river bank downstream from the old tavern's pleasant waterside terrace, parking for cars on either side of the slipway entrance, the wooded island "ait" and, on the opposite bank, the lush green of Kew Gardens. Parallel to the river and overlooking it from across Church Street was a row of oddly assorted old houses—strangely harmonious in their variety—and a pleasant new church in brick with only a weathered stone tower to show for the old church, burnt down some years past.

The best of Church Street, though—or so all four Nicholases agreed—was an attractive white house with a crenellated roof-line and pinnacled corners, entry pillars, and window bays. "The swan that laid our ugly duckling," as Jo put it, brightening noticeably. Stripped clean and bare and made to look even half so graceful, Castle Cox might be tolerably presentable after all.

The first step towards that end, briefly interrupted by a take-away Peking dinner from the Jade House in nearby Upper Square, had been a splendid bonfire built in the cracked basin of a long-dry fishpond. Fed well into the long summer evening with rubbish, wallpaper, buckled mouldings, and the splintered ruins of a large garden lath-house, it sank at last into a glowing ash heap, a rose of light cupped in the dark, warm ring of trees and house.

24

The family sat around it to drink hot chocolate and sing, half mockingly, half seriously, "There's A Long, Long Trail A-Winding," "Memories," and "We All Go The Same Way Home."

A good day. The best ever.

It was only slowly that the sound drifted into Roger's dream like thin, chill tendrils of river-fog seeping into a house on an early autumn morning until room after room grows grey. A low, mournful sound, it came and went and came again. A night-bird, Roger thought at first, knowing nothing of night-birds. But now and again it rose and fell more raggedly than birdsong, a ravelled thread of grief wavering, not out in the pale summer night, but in the house behind him. Roger turned, suddenly frightened, and padded softly to the door into the hall to ease it open.

It had to be Jo crying. Or Pippa. But even as he tiptoed to the far end of the hall he knew it was not Pippa, and when he put his ear to her door he heard nothing. The low, uneven weeping sounded like no child's, but the exhausted, despairing keening of a man or woman, muffled by thick walls and a heavy door. Jo. Roger leaned against the damp plaster of the wall and trembled uncontrollably.

How could they have fought again? How could they, after such a day? It was never easy to know when they were at odds. Their habit of quoting from plays at the drop of a hat gave them a language full of allusion and double meaning. What was said was clear enough, but Roger sometimes sensed that what was meant lay hidden behind the words, perhaps in the characters who spoke them in the play. There had been a moment that afternoon downstairs in the front room—but it had passed so quickly....

Numb with disappointment, Roger felt his way back down the dark hall, to be brought up short before the door to the front bedroom Tony and Jo shared. He meant to hurry past, not wanting to hear—what? low anger, a bitter wrangling?—but he was caught and held.

By silence.

And the grieving that had been everywhere and nowhere now seemed to come from across the hall and down, next to his own room, in the master bedroom Tony and Jo had decided not to use because of the risk of falling plaster. Terrified, Roger had almost gained the safety of his own door when the grieving died into a dry sobbing and a halting whisper. Against his will his eyes were drawn to the open door. The room was empty, bleached pale by moonlight.

And in the empty, moonlit room a voice mourned, *Ah Kitten, why? Cruel, cruel Puss to use me so.*

A man's voice.

tis but our fantafie

IN HIS DREAM THE SOUND OF LAP-
ping water came first to Roger through the
dusk, and then the voice. *Jack? I've not seen
the lad. But if you find him at home, mind you send him
along to us at Brentford for a day or two. You'll want a
chance to woo your pretty wife awhile. We'll keep him
out of mischief until Monday's gathering at Mortlake.*

The voice was clear and warm, yet distant, as if heard
down the length of a long, narrow corridor, and after it
died away there was only a dim confusion of sound:
shouts, the creaking of wood and muffled stamp of horses,
curses and whinnyings, and under it all the steady lap of
water.

27

Then torches were kindled in the half-dark and set in iron standards atop a wall, and Roger saw that the wall was only the top of a row of heavy pilings, a palisade against the river, and that in the middle of its length a broad stone stair stepped down into the shimmering water. Boats crowded at its foot and Roger saw that one, larger, broad-beamed, almost a barge, was half loaded with a strange cargo—among other things, a bedstead, two painted wooden apple trees, an altar, and a gilt throne. Chained and padlocked chests, heavy boxes, and canvas-wrapped rolls six or eight feet long and thick as a man's thigh were handed from the wagons down the stairs to the watermen. As each of the smaller boats crowding close around took on its passenger or two, oarsmen un-shipped their oars and fended off from the bankside, heading upstream with the rising tide. They went, passing into shadows all the deeper for the yellow pinpricks of light strung in clusters along the far bank.

And then it seemed to Roger that the torches grew dim. Of the man who had spoken he saw only a blurred shape descending the water stairs, arm raised in farewell. The gesture was returned from a narrow boat in which an oars-man pulled and a cloaked passenger sat in the upholstered seat facing him. A passenger somehow familiar. . . .

Light, more light! Torches here! Roger heard someone shout. But the shout fell away into the heavy air like a whisper, and as the narrow boat slid through the river shadows into emptiness Roger turned and twisted, strug-gling towards the light and the fading dream.

Roger woke with a start and the dream drained away like water through sand. The sleeping bag was twisted around his chest and knees. All of his windows were wide open and through the one opening out over the green garage roof, the sun rising above Syon Park glittered through the trees. From the window overlooking the back garden came the aroma of bacon frying. For a long, blank moment Roger could not think where he was; but then the bare room, the gaping ceiling and patch of rotted floor dawned on him, and he scrambled out of the sleeping bag so eagerly that the low camp bed tipped over on its side and gave him a sharp crack on the elbow. He hardly noticed, but headed, shivering, for the rear window.

The long shadow of the house lay across the tangled back garden, but below, at the corner of the old kitchen areaway, Bast lay stretched on his back in the one shaft of sunlight. Beyond, down along the garden wall, Roger caught a glimpse of his father's dark head moving along a shaggy row of box trees. Directly below and to Roger's right, on the patch of terrace at the foot of the French-door steps, Jo had set up the camp stove and was turning bacon in the frying pan.

It was too chilly still to stand watching. Roger rooted in his rucksack and brought out his brightest T-shirt, a splintered explosion of colour Alan's Jemmy had hand-dyed in what she called her "Blast" style. Because it looked so alarmingly violent on an empty stomach and wasn't really warm enough, he pulled on over it his old green cotton polo-neck and hurried down the hall to the stairs at the far end.

Breakfast was already in mid-career in the room looking out on the back garden. A new and larger table had been contrived by setting one end of a dingy yellow door on one shelf of the cupboard next to the kitchen stairway, and the other end on yesterday's tea chest. Pippa sat in the doorway at the top of the garden stairs, wiping clean her eggy plate with a piece of toast. "Morning," she mumbled, her mouth full.

"And a very good morning to you and the whole gorgeous world," said Roger, striking a flamboyant pose of welcome to the day. "Anybody know what time it is?"

Jo, still in her monk's-robe dressing gown, peered indoors from her post at the stove. " 'Who is't that greets great morning with a splendour like the sun's?' Our Roger? Wonder of wonders! And it's eight. On the dot. Bacon?"

"Yes, please." Roger cut himself a generous doorstep of bread and clattered down the iron steps past Pippa. "Is there room on there to toast this?"

Jo moved over. "For you, always, sweetie. But you'd better fetch a fork if you don't want to get burnt turning it. I take it you slept well on your bit of canvas?"

"Like the proverbial," Roger said flippantly, armouring himself against taking the affectionate "sweetie" too seriously. After all, it meant no more than any of the vaguely friendly "darlings" and "loves" that were sprinkled through actors' conversation like raisins in a fruitcake. He bounded back up the steps as Pippa shrank aside, then returned, fork in hand, to hesitate frowning in the doorway. "At least. . . . Actually, I was having a peculiar dream just before I woke up, but I can't remember what it was."

Pippa carefully set her plate behind her. "You didn't hear anything last night?" she asked casually.

Jo's head half turned. Even in the shapeless robe her body seemed arrested, listening, like a bird frozen on one foot.

Roger frowned, then paled, remembering. "Why?" he countered. "Did you?"

"Maybe. I *thought* so. Like somebody crying, almost. I wanted to get up and go see, but Sammy was petrified, and old Bast jumped on my stomach and hissed like anything every time I tried to get out from under. Mama heard it too."

"*Did* you, Jo?"

Jo, turning, nodded. "I take it that you did too."

Roger avoided meeting her eyes. "I thought it was—the animals, maybe. I got up and listened at the doors."

" 'Doors' plural?" Jo regarded him gravely. The shadows under Roger's eyes had worried her for weeks and this morning, if anything, they were darker. "Ours too?"

"I thought you and Pa might be having a f-fight," Roger said lightly, as if the possibility held little interest. But he felt one eyelid begin to tic nervously and turned away with a shrug, so that Jo would not notice.

"I see. We weren't, though. And even when we *do*, it's usually no great matter. You—" She broke off as Tony appeared over by the north-west fence and came, plate in hand, picking his way through the brambles. "Your father slept like the dead through it all. Didn't hear a thing."

"The big bedroom. It came from there." Roger went down to turn his toast and said hesitantly, "It sounds silly in broad daylight, but it sounded like someone all broken up over a lost cat. A kitten or a cat."

"I'm disappointed in you, Rog." Tony came to peer at the bacon. "A little night breeze moans through that colander of a roof, and you begin coining ghosts. Not that we're ill-placed for it," he added with a ghoulish waggle of eyebrows and a nod in the direction of the river. "We're bang up against the churchyard on that side." Spearing the lone slice of toast with his fork, he held it out to Jo on his plate. "None of your brittle, dried-up rashers, please. The three fatty ones will do nicely."

"Hey, that was *my* toast," Roger objected.

His father forked the three pieces of bacon one on top of the other, bent the toast to make a sandwich of sorts, and took a crafty bite before saying, perfectly convincingly, "Yours? Sorry, Rog, I didn't realize. Here, you have it."

Roger's grimace at the indigestible-looking sandwich became a reluctant grin. "No, thanks. I like bacon Jo's way, crisp."

"All right." Tony took another bite. "But I will cut you some more bread. Coffee in on the table, Jo?"

"In the thermos."

A moment later Tony tossed two slices of bread out to Roger, who placed them on the grill and this time kept an eye on them. When his own bacon sandwich was built, he went in search of milk. The jug was on the door-table, and after pouring himself a mugful he went to sit on the step beside Pippa. Jo in turn drifted off into the garden, bearing with her on a plate all the rest of the bacon. Behind, in the dining-room, Tony prowled along the fireplace wall, poking, knocking, and prodding.

"The panelling's buckled well away from the chimney up there," he observed, squinting at the cracked cornice and the ugly brown water stain on the ceiling that spread in a ragged semi-circle out from the fireplace wall. "Those floorboards just above must be rotten through. If I thought we could trust the chimney, I'd rip this old gas fire out of here and build a proper fire—start drying things out—but

I haven't seen anything we could use as a grate. Any ideas?"

Roger shrugged, not bothering to turn. "Not unless we have the electricity turned on and buy some electric fires."

"Too late. The Electricity Board won't be taking work orders on a Saturday morning. I suppose," Tony muttered, squatting down on his heels to inspect the dust-clogged gas fire. "We could buy a grate. The local hardware shop might have one or two stored away. Hah! This thing seems to have been very thoroughly disconnected. No gas inlet pipe at all."

Roger and Pippa turned to see the old cage-fronted gas fire pull free at Tony's tug and topple on its face with a tinkle of shattering ceramic heating elements. Tony stuck his head into the empty blackened fireplace and gave the soot a jab with the edge of his tin plate. "Iron. Looks like one of those fancy old Victorian items. Pity the face has been covered up with this panelling. Some of them are quite ornate. Made to be framed by the mantel surround and overmantel."

Pippa helped herself to bread and jam and came to look. "Why not pull it off, then?" she touched the panelling gingerly. "It's ugly. The paint's all crackled."

"Probably means the wood's damp right through." Still squatting, Tony peered upward speculatively. "I think you're right, Pips. But it'll take some tools. A crowbar and claw hammer to begin with. I'm going out for the newspapers anyway, so I'll look for an ironmonger's while I'm at it. We can pick up grates for this fireplace and the front room, and for the two upstairs if there are any to be had. What I'll need first, Pips, is the steel tape measure from the tool box in the back of the car, to get the width of this thing. it's probably at the very bottom, in with the sockets and what-nots." He stood and fished the car keys from his pocket.

Roger recognized the glint in his father's eye and almost choked on the last of his milk. It was the intense, abstracted gleam that appeared when Tony was first concentrating his way into the depths of a new role. He had wandered around like that for two weeks upon learning that he was to take over as Hamlet for two months of this latest run of last year's very successful production. Roger rose and walked casually to the makeshift table, setting his mug and plate down with deliberate care. If his father had that look now, it could mean only one thing: he was caught.

"It won't do much good, will it?" Roger asked lightly. "Not for just two days."

"What?" Tony said vaguely. Drawing back a yard or so, he squinted at the fireplace wall. "We might even cheat a little, make it look a bit older. Regency instead of early Victorian. 'Early Brighton Pavilion.' Not the best of periods for claiming a ghost, but it could be equally entertaining." He frowned. "You're right about the fires. They won't be enough. On Monday we'll have to see about having the electricity laid on. No telling how long a wait we'll have before it's connected. For now you'd better come with me in search of the next best thing."

Roger almost held his breath. "But we have to go home tomorrow night. You have a rehearsal call Monday morning, and there's my cello lesson."

Tony shrugged. "No reason Jo can't stay. She's not working now. Not until the middle of next month. And once I've smoothed out a few rough spots in this *Hamlet*,

I can begin commuting. I can come down after the Wednesday matinee anyway. We're not on again until Saturday night. Of course," he added, "if you object to roughing it. . . ."

Roger grinned at his father's back. "Are we staying for *good*, then?"

"As if you didn't know," Tony drawled, turning to fix on Roger a scowl of friendly malice. "It's what you counted on, wasn't it? 'Once through that front door and the old man's stuck'?"

"Hoo-*ee*!"

Roger let out a wild whoop and leapt out and down the iron garden steps to meet Jo, emerging from the brambles, and whirl her in a dizzy circle.

"We're staying! Pa said so. We're *staying*!"

8 Is not this something more then phantasie?

O EYED THE SACK OF COAL DOUBT-fully. "Are you sure it's *safe* to build a fire in there?" she asked mildly. "If that gas heater is as ancient as it looks, this chimney hasn't been used for years. For all we know it's stuffed full of antique birds' nests, and the first spark will burn the house down around our ears."

Tony sat back on his heels to scowl at the half-built fire in the new grate, and then at Jo. "Have you any idea how far we had to go for coals in August? Hounslow!"

"It's not all that far," Jo said placidly. "I'm sorry I didn't think to ask before, though. I'm surprised I thought of it at all, seeing as I've never had a real fire-place. It just seemed. . . ."

"I know. 'Logical,' " Tony drawled. "O.K., Roger, out it comes."

Together they lifted out the half-filled grate and set it in the nearest corner. "Pa," Roger asked suddenly, "what about the steel measuring tape?"

"What about it?"

"It's a long one. Twelve feet. Couldn't we feed it up the opening and try twisting it around? Like one of those Dyno-Rod or Roto-Rooter cables for blocked drains? If it won't go up, we'll know it's blocked."

"Not a bad idea. And if it does clear, we can try the same with the fireplace above. The chimney pots are probably more than another twelve feet above that, but if it's clear that far, we can burn a sheet or so of newspaper to see whether it draws. Now, where did I put the blasted tape?"

"You'll make an awful mess," Jo warned. "Soot all over the place. I can move the food cartons and the picnic gear, but if you don't want to ruin your clothes, you'll put on your bathing shorts. Believe it or not, there's an old tin bathtub in that cubbyhole off the back end of the garage. If you get too grubby you can toss a coin for who gets the bathroom, and who gets a tin tub down in the kitchen."

"And cold water in both of them." Roger shuddered as he said it, and Tony made a face at the prospect.

"She may be right. We'll give it a short test poke to see if it's worth it, shall we?" Tony reached for the unread *Times* and *Guardian* and filched the business sections to spread on the hearth and the floor round it. It took a bit of a struggle to open the damper once he located it; then, pulling out a three foot length of the tape and locking it, Tony knelt sideways and pushed it up into the dark opening. A short way in, it stopped, and when he tried to force it through the obstruction, it bent with a metallic twang and sent down a small shower of soot.

"Fourteen inches?" Tony grunted. "Some chimney!"

"It might be a bend in the flue," Roger suggested.

"Not that much of a bend. Has to be a right angle." Tony pulled out the measure and rolled his shirt sleeves well above the elbow. With his right hand he groped upward through the opening. "Hah! You're right at that. It does angle upward, but only barely." He brought his grimy forearm out with a frown. "And it's smooth, except for the soot. Feels more like a stove pipe than a proper chimney. Here, let's have that measure again."

Guiding the steel ribbon past the sharp angle in the flue, he fed more and more of its length into the black hole. At last it met some resistance, but at the next insistent push twanged dimly and moved on reluctantly, as if it had rounded another corner. Then it jammed and could be forced no further. Carefully, Tony pulled it down to the second bend and took hold of the tape at the flue opening with thumb and forefinger to mark the length.

"What is it?" Roger was excited by the intent frown on his father's face. Jo, watching idly, noticed with some surprise that Tony's eyes, like Roger's, were underlined with shadow. Odd, when he had slept well. It made the two of them, crouched before the fireplace, look strangely more like brothers than father and son.

"I'm not sure," Tony said slowly. He pulled the tape free to have a look at the number beside his grimy thumb.

Five feet, it read. "Allowing for the straight-up bit, it looks as if for the first four feet the blasted thing aims for the stair landing in the hall, not for the roof. *Then* it turns up." He sat back on his heels.

"Does that mean anything?" Pippa asked for all of them.

"One thing at least," Tony said. "This can't be the original fireplace. It must be set at the front of a deeper one. Deeper and older. Well, well, well!" His voice softened to a whisper.

"It would fit," Jo said slowly. "At least, the house looks as if it's been seriously messed about at some point. Do you suppose we have an eighteenth-century swan lurking inside our mucky duckling?"

"Only one way to find out." Tony straightened purposefully, looked at his blackened hands, and crossed to the kitchen stairs. In a few moments he emerged again, wiping them dry on the Dutch handkerchief he wore as a neck-scarf. "Now. Where's our new crowbar?"

Jo looked a little worried. "You're not going to do anything drastic, are you?" But as Roger produced the short chisel-ended iron bar, her eybrows quirked up in a caricature of resignation. "You are going to do something drastic. And if you're wrong, it will probably cost a packet to put it right again. I'll end up giving up my long holiday, and having to do that ITV play after all."

"Oh, do shut up," Tony growled good-humouredly. Lifting the now-clear makeshift table free of the shelf of the middle wall cupboard, he propped it up and pulled the upended tea case across to the hearth. Testing first to see that it would bear his weight, he climbed onto it, carefully placing his feet near opposite corners. The wedge-end of the crowbar he jammed forcibly into the right-of-centre seam high on the painted panelling near where the damp had buckled it out from the cornice, but below the worst of the water stain. It went in with a soft *thwump*!

"Rotten." Tony's grimace was gleeful as he worked the bar in and leftward under the panel until he had leverage. With a slow, careful outward pressure he pried until the top of the central panel groaned outward with a soft, ripping sound. Pippa, who had temporarily lost interest when the chimney failed to produce birds' nests or bat skeletons, was suddenly on the spot with a tin of Old El Paso tortillas to wedge behind the loosened panel. Roger shoved the tea case aside after his father climbed down, and held his breath as the crowbar bit into the lower seam. The wood there was not rotten, and it was only after a lot of patient prying back and forth and not-so-patient commentary, that the bar was worked in far enough for one great wrench.

"Out of the way, you lot," Tony grated.

His audience scattered. The panel, when it gave, sprang loose with an explosion as sharp as a rifle shot. It flew against the opposite wall with a noisy clatter and only narrowly missed shattering the panes of the nearest French door. The tortilla tin caromed across the room and rolled down the kitchen stairs.

Where the panel had been, a four foot width of badly stained plaster extended downward to slightly below shoulder height. The space from there to the top of the inset iron fireplace had been completely filled in with unmortared brick.

Jo whistled softly. "Well, well, a cigar for the gentleman." But then her voice sharpened in alarm. "Tony? What is it?"

"Pa? Are you all right" Roger crossed quickly from the front room doorway.

Tony, suddenly pale, had turned to press his forehead against the cool plaster. After a moment he mumbled, "I'm all right," and brushed the crumbled plaster from his brow. "Things slipped out of focus for a moment. Gave me a bit of a fright, that's all."

Roger let go of his father's arm reluctantly. "You're sure?"

"I'll make you a cup of tea," Jo said quietly.

"Thanks." Tony shook his head as if to clear it and retrieved the crowbar from the floor. "Now then," he said firmly. "Let us see whether it's a swan or a flat-footed bustard we're landed with. This plaster is what I'd call 'dead.' It's been pretty coarse stuff to begin with, and the water seepage has finished it." He raked the crowbar down its surface, cutting into it as if it were soft chalk.

But a foot above the brick fill the biting iron rang against stone.

Roger's eyes met his father's for one frozen moment, and the crowbar dropped to the floor with a clatter. Tony pulled out his pocket knife, and Roger grabbed the kitchen knife Pippa fetched from the cupboard. When Jo reappeared from the terrace with a steaming mug of tea, they had chipped free of plaster the central portion of a shallow arch of stone.

"Looks like we really have something," Tony exulted as he scraped carefully at the plaster imbedded in the carving in the stone.

Bit by bit his knife revealed a simple strapwork knot

cut into the arch's apex. In the knot's centre was the letter *G*, and numbers set between the corners of the knot appeared to spell out a date.

"Am I crazy," Tony whispered incredulously, "or does that say *1603*?"

It was almost two o'clock before the Nicholases (and Sammy), dusty-haired and happy, straggled down to the Apprentice for a lunch of bread and cheese on the crowded terrace at the river's edge. They were oblivious to the faintly ghostly appearance they presented in the midday sun in their dusting of plaster, and quite unaware of the open curiosity of children and the amused recognition of a few of the adults. Heads together over the table, they made a list of items they would need: wood scrapers to clean the plaster from the oak wainscoting that was the original facing of the chimney wall, stiff nylon brushes for the fine work, a wire one for the wide stone arch, bucket and sponge mop—and a proper wrecking bar. While Jo added to the list of foodstuffs they would need if they were to stay over for Sunday supper and Monday breakfast, Tony edged back into the crowded pub for a second pint of bitters and a few moments on the telephone to Alan Collet.

"Could you get hold of him?" Jo asked when they met outside the door nearest the parking area and made their way across Church Street.

"No problem. He was in the middle of making up for this afternoon's performance and didn't quite appreciate the interruption, but he did come to the phone. He'll be here for brunch tomorrow at eleven and, yes, he's bringing our junior architect."

"Jemima!" Pippa crowed.

"Jemima. They won't stay the night, though. She has to catch an early train back to Cambridge Monday morning."

"Let's hope she knows her regional architectural history well enough to tell me how to start tracking down the tale of Castle Cox," Jo remarked as she and Tony rounded the curve in the footpath past the church. Pippa and Roger were already far ahead. "I *do* wish Rog had some friends his own age," Jo added unexpectedly.

Tony seemed startled. "Hasn't he? He always seems to be busy enough."

"With *us*. When we're on hand. Or swimming, or off on his own at a cricket match. *Or* lugging his blessed cello off to a lesson with that utter zero of an Albert Cluck."

"*Clock*, chucklehead." Tony put an arm around her shoulders and drew hers around his waist. "I shouldn't worry. Old Roger's used to looking after himself. After all, he used to look after *me* until you took the job on. No, he'll be turning up with a girl friend one of these days, and you'll go tacking off in the other direction."

"Umm. Perhaps. But I do wish he didn't tread through

life so warily. You'd think the Great Cake of the Universe was going to fall if he put a foot wrong."

"*Roger?* Don't be silly," Tony scoffed. He gave her an affectionate squeeze and when they turned in at their own drive, added a kiss that effectively put Roger out of her mind.

By teatime the shopping was done, the whole of the original fireplace wall was exposed, the iron Victorian fireplace dragged clear and toppled down the steps into the garden (where it shattered a terrace paving stone), and the insulating bricks chucked over the railing at the side of the garden stairs to be stacked at leisure. There was still a great deal more to be done in the way of cleaning—the wainscoting was grey with soaked-in plaster and some mildew—but they could sit on the floor with buttered raisin bread and mugs of milk or tea and contemplate the patterned wall and the graceful flattened arch of stone enclosing a deep, fire-blackened fireplace some four feet high and seven wide.

"Next," Tony said with a determined gleam in his eye, "we measure the entire house, outside and in, to give us some idea of what else might be lurking inside the walls of our plaster castle. Pips, you're the artist. Rog and I can measure and you can put it down on paper. I said right from the first that the proportions were all wrong, didn't I? I'll wager that in every case it's because something has been tacked on or covered over. We, my dears, are going to pare it down to its seventeenth-century heart."

When Roger drifted into sleep at last, he fell to dreaming of tape measures that wrapped themselves around corners and slithered up and down walls like flat, silver snakes. *Seventeen feet, two-and-a-quarter inches,* they hissed. *Fifty-four feet and half an inch. Nine feet precisely.*

When you touched a finger to their backs, you felt a ripple, like a pulse, almost, and when their silver tongues whispered out they sighed *Cruel, cruel Roger to use me so.* Unreasonably—he knew it was nonsensical—Roger began to be afraid of what they might measure out: a house hidden within a house, meanings hidden in words, feelings bravely tricked out in smiles. *Ah Kitten, why?* whispered one as it wrapped round his ankle and set to work to measure him.

Roger came half awake with a start, the sensation of an icy-cold band round his ankle so real that he lay paralysed, his heart racing, until it died away. *It-was-only-a-dream,* his mind said, the message shaping itself in some far-off corner and floating towards him. The words were as hard to capture as soap bubbles. *Dream?* His mind flickered more sharply. Was he awake now, then? His body was a heavy weight, thick, inert as clay; and as his mind struggled towards the surface, his body lay below, dreaming its own dream, like a rock lying on its side in the river bed. *Move,* he commanded. *Stretch.* But it would not. *Puss? Kitten? Who were they?*

In the next room he heard a muffled crash, then the creak and slam of what might have been a cupboard door opening and shutting. No grieving. Only angry footsteps, and a heavy door wrenched open. *Look. See. Who's there?* Roger's brain signalled frantically, and after an endless time his eyelids dragged open and he saw the moonlit rooms. Both. For there were two of them: his

45

own, bare and ugly, and under it—within it?—not a room, but a wainscoted passageway and the heavy, carved balustrade of a broad stairwell, shimmering half-seen, like a darkly lit stage setting behind a heavy scrim.

Roger blinked heavily. The illusion did not go away; and he could not move his head even to see the downward flight of stairs that must lie at his bed's foot. In that room within his own—that wide upper landing—no hall doorway opened opposite the window at his back. A shadowy carved chest stood against a wall just there, an empty candlestick atop it. And the pale yellow light spilling across the floor not seven feet from Roger's numb gaze came from the empty master bedroom. Through a door that was-not-there.

From that not-room, a man burst into the passageway to stand half dazed, candlestick in hand. He was tall and dark and, but for the face, might have been Tony standing there, costumed for some play in doublet, trunk hose, and half-cloak, a plumed hat under his arm. But the face was nothing like. It was a good enough face, but the grief and anger wavering there had made it ugly. The man's right hand, white-knuckled, gripped the haft of the poniard that hung on a gilt and silver chain from his belt. Roger, frozen fast, saw every link of the chain, every point of lace edging the falling bands at his neck.

Then, abruptly, the man moved, hurling himself towards the stair and passing out of Roger's view. He was gone, but the sound of footsteps pelting down and the thud of a heavy outer door were a long time dying.

Move. Wake up. Stop the dream. Blood thrummed in Roger's ears like deep, plucked bass notes on a cello, an underwater sound, until the stone that was his body stirred and stretched and sat up shivering, half naked, in the wash of moonlight through the open window.

The terrifying thing was that he knew he had been awake all the time.

8 It would haue much a maz'd you

PIPPA CAME OUT OF HER ROOM IN shorts and a Snoopy T-shirt just as Roger started down the stairs. "I heard it again last night," she said in a hushed, conspiratorial voice. "Did you? Are you going to tell them?"

Roger kept ahead on the way down, careful not to meet those curious, excited eyes. "No. I was too tired to stay awake," he said shortly. "Anyway, Pa's right. An old house with chimneys and a Swiss-cheese roof can make as many sounds as an organ."

He had decided in the middle of the night, after two sleepless hours, to say nothing of what he had seen. His father would greet such a tale with impatience or irritation or, worse, amusement masked by a caricature of concern. "Ought we to try communicating with this antique gentleman? We could have a go at table-rapping, but we haven't a proper table. Do you reckon he would settle for our door?" Jo might be more open-minded, but she would be bound to be uneasy at the prospect—however doubtful—of sharing premises with a ghost. Pippa? Well, Pippa would probably see a ghost as one more creature in need of aid and comfort, so she would be no problem. But for Tony and Jo, it would be better if they were a lot more deeply involved in re-doing the house before they found out. Time enough when the roof was repaired and they moved across the hall into the master bedroom. Besides, there was always the possibility that when he—"it"?— had slammed out of the house last night, he had gone for good.

At the bottom of the stairs Roger turned to Pippa to ask with casual curiosity, "What was it you thought you heard?"

"Like before, only not so long. Are you sure you didn't hear anything?"

"I said I didn't," Roger answered impatiently, but half-way along the hall he slowed. "Why? You didn't *see* something, did you?"

"No. Not exactly." Pippa frowned. "But I put Sammy and Bast to bed in their baskets so they wouldn't sit all over me if I wanted to get up. And when I heard whatever-it-was I got up and went down the hall to where it was coming from."

"But you didn't see anything?"

Pippa shook her head. "No. And that was funny too.

Funny-peculiar, I mean. *My* room was all moonlighty, but I could hardly see into the big room at all. It was all murky, like there was a wall of something across the doorway. It was so spooky I ran and got into bed and zipped the sleeping bag clear up over my head."

A wall. There might very well have been a wall, Roger thought. The old house and Castle Cox seemed to differ in more ways than one. "You must have been dreaming," he told Pippa offhandedly. Taking hold of her lopsided ponytail, he neatly refastened it and gave it a parting tug. "Where's Sammy?"

"Upstairs with his basket door open. I told him he'd have to come down on his own this morning," she said primly and went on in to breakfast.

Tony was there, in a foul temper, complaining about the state of his egg and accusing Jo of having boiled the coffee. He looked as haggard as if he had sat up half the night.

"Cooking on that thing *is* a little unpredictable," Jo granted. "But one more word and you're on your own tomorrow morning. I am sorry about the egg, but the coffee most assuredly did not boil. That sour taste is last night's celebration come back to haunt you."

"Two pints of beer do not make a celebration," Tony snapped.

"Two?"

"Well then, three," he growled. "And this morning I mean to celebrate my early Jacobean house by ringing friend Collet and telling him to stay at home."

"You can't," Jo said. She stilled Roger's threatened protest with a look. "Not before twelve, and they'll be here before then."

"I needn't wait until the pub opens to phone. There'll be

a kiosk somewhere. Dammit, there's too much to do, and I don't feel up to Alan's unbridled cheerfulness on top of it all." Tony snatched up an orange and headed for the French doors.

"Temper, temper! And hours too late," said a disembodied voice.

Pippa was closest to the front door. "It's Alan!" she announced through a mouthful of toast. Swallowing quickly, she demanded, "Where's Jemima?"

Alan Collet stood just outside a front room window, his chin on the window sill. A shaft of morning sunlight fell full on his blond hair and the effect was startling, as if his head were a round golden ornament, grinning and grotesque, left there by a passing practical joker. "Jemmy? She's coming in at the front door and I am right behind her." He vanished.

By the time Alan and Jemima appeared in the diningroom doorway, Tony had dredged up a martyred smile from somewhere. Jo floated up from the terrace, arms wide in welcome. "Don't mind the pet bear," she said. "It's got a sore head."

"Yes, but Bear wants a kiss," Tony said, and bent to claim one from Jemima. "There, Rog. Beat you to it."

Roger's face flamed, but it amounted to a dare and so he said, " 'Morning, Jemmy," and planted a quick kiss at the corner of her mouth.

Jemima was special: small, blonde and blue-eyed, she made up in earnestness for Alan's flamboyant and sometimes highly irritating good cheer. Not that she was any less fun-loving, but she did take everything and everyone seriously, and for this children in particular, and everyone in general, loved her. "Tell me more," she always said, as if she didn't know enough already to make Roger's

51

head swim. Alan, like Tony a member of the National Theatre Company, had met Jemima in 1969 at a large, anonymous party after the formal cornerstone-laying at the company's new Bankside site. Jemima had, Roger understood, something minor to do with the rough architectural drawings for the new complex. "Inking in the spelling corrections," she claimed. It *might* have been true.

"Awful of us to appear so hard upon your rising," Alan observed blithely, "but Jemmy's been at me like a dog at a flea from the moment I told her about your tarted-up Tudor chimney. If you'll settle for giving us breakfast instead of brunch, we'll stand you to a lunch out. Deal?"

"Deal," Jo agreed readily.

Tony, still looking distinctly bleary, pressed his fingers to his temples. "Tudor? You're right, 1603 could be either Tudor or Jacobean, couldn't it? 'Tudor' sounds much the better."

Jemima was already on her knees inside the fireplace. "Call it 'Elizabethan'—it's that even if it was finished after Queen Bess died that March. Jacobean styles were a while in growing—they didn't come south from Scotland in King Jamie's baggage." She scrambled out. "Your fireplace *is* splendid. How did you find it out? Tell me everything!"

When they had, Pippa's sketchbook with the measurements and rough floor plans was produced and passed around with the bacon and eggs and coffee. Jemima pored over it, nodding like an eager dippy-bird. "Oh yes, I think so. Yes. Oh, yes."

"Yes what?" demanded Pippa, not one to hold her breath for long. Sammy, who had found his way downstairs to her shoulder, peered at the drawings too.

"Yes, I think I can see something of the shape of the original house. Something seems to be missing, but my guess is that even more has been tacked on. Look." On a fresh page she quickly sketched out a more accurate plan of the ground-floor arrangement, shading in the fireplace and wall areas of the two larger rooms. "Here and here, you see..." Jemima pointed to the lines representing the rear wall with the French doors, and the interior wall parallel to it. "Here are two walls of the same thickness, but the front wall appears by your measurements to be much lighter. Now you almost never see that heavy an interior wall in a small house even if it is a bearing wall. My guess is that this wing of the house originally looked like...this. The room we're in would have been the 'hall,' the main room." She handed a second sketch across the door-table.

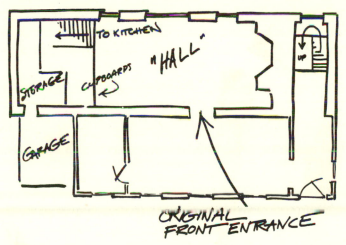

"That might have been the front wall of the house?" Tony asked blankly. "The one Alan and his breakfast are propping up?"

53

Alan was sitting beside the door into the front room with his back against the wall. He turned to look at the doorway. "It is a bit thick, isn't it? Makes a nice effect with the steps coming up, though. You wouldn't want to go and knock the front rooms off, would you? I mean, restoration is all very well, but that's a bit much."

"Yes," Tony said drily. "A bit."

"But we can look, can't we?" Roger asked anxiously. "Just to know if it's so?"

Jo smiled. "Roger's right. At least *I*'d like to know. What's a little plaster and woodwork in a good cause?"

"Not much," Tony agreed resignedly. "But if you must chip holes in my house, do so gently. My head is already splitting."

"Absolutely. Swear." Alan finished off his coffee and crossed his heart. "We brought some tools down on the off-chance we might be allowed in on the fun. I'll go fetch 'em."

"And I'll get dressed," Jo said, swishing off hastily in her dressing gown.

Among the Sunday papers and gear in the jump-seat of the old MG (the sledge-hammer, Alan insisted, was Jemima's too) was a large pad of drawing paper and a flat case of drawing instruments, so that while Alan and Roger made a timid beginning with hammers and chisels in the front room on a patch of plaster near the doorway, Jemima set about translating the measurements Tony and Jo and the children had made into more precise ground plans.

"Pa?" Roger's croak came after only ten minutes. "Pips, where's Pa?"

"He's outside. What've you found?" Pippa came plunging down the two steps from the dining room. "That's it, isn't it? The old house?" At Alan's nod Pippa raced for the nearest window to shriek, "Tony? *Daddy?* They found it!"

Tony, sprawled in one of the lawn chairs in a patch of sunshine in the middle of the driveway, raised the section of the *Observer* that covered his face and blinked. "*Daddy?* Good heavens, has it come to that? Well, what have they found?"

"The front of the house!"

That brought him out of his chair in a hurry.

What Roger and Alan had found beneath the thick plaster was a brick wall—or the first small patch of it. A brisk rubbing with the wire pot-brush used on the stone fireplace brought one brick in the herringbone pattern alive in a warm, dark red that Jemima pronounced undoubtedly Elizabethan. Tony was quite revived.

Jemima went to stand between the two front windows for a wider view of the wall and suggested that not only could the door between the two rooms have been the principal entrance of the early house, but the built-in glass-fronted book cases might have been fitted into the original window openings. Tony would have taken the sledge-hammer to them on the instant but held off at Jo's protest that the doors and shelves were well worth salvaging.

"The door. Do the door first," Pippa proposed, enjoying this grown-up game wholeheartedly.

"I don't know," Roger said nervously. He was a little wary of the high enthusiasm Tony and Alan looked like working up between them. He peered up at the heavy, ornate lintel that repeated along its top the castle crenellations of the house's roofline. "It looks pretty solid."

Alan tapped up and down the frame with the hammer. "Looks and is. It doesn't actually have to *be* solid, though. Might just be good solid workmanship. Let's have a go."

"I think you're out of your tiny mind. *But*—" Tony took a deep breath. "Where's the wrecking bar?"

After the first long shard of wood ripped off, leaving an ugly scar, there was a bad five minutes during which it began to look as if they had made a terrible mistake. Jo covered her eyes. The doorpost would not loosen, and only after several careful cuts had been made with a saw at the top and bottom of the doorframe could the two men, pulling together on the heavy bar, rip the woodwork loose. Roger caught hold of it while they slipped the bar further in. At the chink of metal on stone, Tony's eyes danced.

"Did you hear that?" He panted, "Josie, my puss, I think it's safe to uncover. *Look*."

At the next heave the face of the doorpost ripped away, revealing underneath it a warm expanse of weathered stone. The woodwork was, like the plaster, only a casing, a cold formal mask on a warm, homely face.

"Bingo!" Jo whispered.

Alan, Jemima and the Nicholases, more or less scrubbed clean of plaster, trooped off to lunch at the Apprentice in a high humour. Tony was still a bit hollow-eyed, but cheerfully insisted that his headache had disappeared in the excitement, declaiming with his hand on his heart, " 'I have—as when the sun doth light a storm—buried this sigh in wrinkle of a smile.' " For a while as they worked it had looked as if the great door lintel itself, well out of reach, would have to wait for a ladder, but with each attack on the casings of the doorposts below it had been loosened a little, and in the end toppled free with a great crash while everyone was queued up in the kitchen or bathroom to wash. It left a stone lintel as simply and elegantly arched as the great fireplace, and carved at the centre of that shallow arch was a monogram—TG or GT —bracketed by the numbers of the same date that was carved on the fireplace:

"If you do the work yourselves, the restoration could take two or three years," said Jemima, waving a fork over the remains of her salad. "But then there's no guarantee it wouldn't take almost that long if you had a builder in to do it. The roofing and re-wiring you can't do, of course, but otherwise so long as you don't mind living in a muddle you can save thousands."

"In that case," said Jo, "what do we knock apart next?"

Jemima retrieved her drawing pad from the rosebush's barrel-tub it was propped against and, as Alan cleared the plates away, laid it on the table. "There's something suspicious about your lovely fireplace—there." Her pencil tapped a shaded area. "That's an awfully thick rear chimney wall between the hearth and your stairwell."

Tony leaned back against the terrace railing as if to say, "Come now, this is too much." The look he gave Jemima was skeptical. "Come, Jemmy, not a priest's hole!"

"It could be."

Pippa was lost. "What's a priest's hole?"

"A little secret room made for a Catholic priest to hide

in. Back when the house was built, it was illegal for them to say Mass, and the Puritans wanted all of them shut up in jail—or hung," Tony explained. "But I thought those holes were built with an entrance at the back of the fireplace itself; and ours is solid."

Jemima shook her head earnestly. "Some of them were, yes. But the entrance could just as easily have been from the stair side. Even through a removable stair tread."

Jo finished off her glass of white wine. "I think that Jemima means that we must rip out the staircase next," she drawled.

"*No*," Roger said. The word came out sharply, before he had a chance to think.

"No what?" Alan asked quizzically. "No hole or no rip?"

Roger took a deep breath. "No staircase," he said and pointed to the drawing. "The staircase was over here, at the other end of the house."

"Nonsense," Tony said. "What gave you that idea?"

"Nothing. I just know," Roger said evasively.

Jemima frowned at her floor plan. "It *would* actually make more sense at the south-east end of the house. Having it hidden behind the fireplace doesn't really fit. By your date they had begun to make rather a thing of the gracious stairway. If there was a small room where your stairs are now, that thick chimney wall might simply mean back-to-back fireplaces.

"But there *is* no gracious stairway," Tony pointed out.

"No," Jemima agreed distantly. With an intent little frown she pushed back her chair, tucked the drawing pad under her arm and was off, threading her way among the tables and out onto Church Street. The others followed like the fascinated children of Hamelin. Jo, bringing up the rear of the procession, squeezed between two back-to-back chairs and said airily to the perfect stranger in one of them, "Do excuse us. We have gone completely mad."

Even Roger thought Jemima was being silly about the lost stair. What he had seen (or dreamt, as he had begun to think of it) had taken up almost the whole of his room, leaving only the upper landing—the wide stretch from the present hall door to the window opposite. Certainly now there was nothing in his room but an expanse of floor; but having examined that, Jemima poked around in the kitchen stairway, in the oddly-arranged cupboards beside it, and in the low, dark storage hole off the back of the garage. And grew more excited by the minute.

"Don't you see? It not only *was* here, it *is* here. Or a part of it is. Whatever happened to the original kitchen and pantry wing—fire perhaps—when the new front was added and the cellar enlarged for a kitchen, they dismantled the upper railings and did away with the stairway by flooring the space over. But the rest of it is still here!" She snatched up her black felt pen and began rapidly to sketch a broad half-flight of stairs, a landing along an end wall and an upper flight, roughing in sturdy turned newel posts and balusters and a broad rail.

"Now, look." With a red pen she fitted the outline of the present interior in and around the Elizabethan stair: the odd cupboards that grew deeper as they climbed, the low-ceilinged box room under the landing floor, and the kitchen stair descending below the flight from the landing to the floor above.

Jemima stabbed her pen at the space between the vanished landing and Roger's bedroom floor. "Don't you see yet? *That space is lost.* If that landing isn't in there still, why isn't your box room ceiling ten feet high instead of five? And that sloping alcove on this side of the box room? That has to be a part of the space under the lower stair."

She was right. Roger knew it. And the sketch was such a strange daylight echo of what he had seen by moonlight—the old house shimmering under this one—that excitement swept aside his memory of the violent, unhappy scene he had witnessed on that upper landing.

"Pa? *Please*, Pa?"

Alan picked up the crowbar and caressed it with a grin. "Shall we have a look?"

Tony surveyed the circle of expectant faces. "If someone will fetch me a couple of aspirins first," he said faintly.

"We can start at that rotten spot in my floor," Roger said, plunging through the front room and on upstairs.

It did not take long. Through a hole ripped open in a matter of minutes, the shifting beam of light from an electric torch picked out the broad, dust-thick stairs and, in a dusty cobwebbed jumble on the landing, the dismantled upper railings, newel post, and balusters.

"Gosh, what's Roger going to do for a bedroom now?" Pippa asked.

With two-thirds of his bedroom floor ripped up, Roger elected to bed down in the small room Tony had at first mistaken for the kitchen. He was certainly not about to sleep in the master bedroom and chance meeting his apparition again. Vision or ghost, he had actually seen something, and whether he had been dreaming or waking seemed beside the point so long as a part of it had proved to be true. In the newer part of the house he might get a good night's rest.

Even so, it was not easy to fall asleep. For a while Roger read the colour sections of the Sunday papers by flashlight in his sleeping bag. Alan had brought them, and after a long day, gone home having had no chance to read even the headlines. Roger, when he had finished reading, lay for a long time in the dark thinking about the beautiful lower stair with the sweep of its wide oak steps, the heavy carved newel posts and turned balusters, and the fine, broad rail. Grime and all, it was beautiful. And yet....

Roger could not have said when he slipped off to sleep, but it was three by his watch when he was wakened by a loud knocking at the front door, and the reflection on his wall of a light being shone in at the front windows. He sat up, for a moment bewildered, and then stumbled into the front room. Through the window he saw the glow of the POLICE sign atop a small car, and a tall, dark figure in the driveway flashing his light at the windows to attract attention. Roger was still so dazed with sleep that it was another moment before he realized that the knocking at the door ought to be answered. In the dark hall he fumbled at the lock and finally managed to open the door.

A second tall shadow in the shape of a uniformed police constable stood on the doorstep and flashed a light on him briefly. "Police, son. I'm sorry to disturb you, but does an Anthony Charles Nicholas live here?"

"Yes." Roger blinked. "My dad. But—do you want me to get him out of bed?"

"No." The constable sounded faintly amused. "We

would prefer that you put him back into it."

Roger was still trying to grasp what he meant when Jo, still half asleep, came teetering down the dark stairs and groped her way to the door and the beam of light.

"Tony? Didn't Tony come down? What's happened?"

"Mrs. Nicholas? It's quite all right," the tall shadow soothed. "We have him in the car."

"In the—" Jo was as blank as Roger.

"He's been sleepwalking, I'm afraid. We had a report from a resident and came along to the moorings down by the Apprentice. We found him in a rowboat belonging to one of the cruisers, fast asleep with his eyes open, and about to cast off and row down the Thames. Fast asleep."

8 There is a play to night

ND I SAID I MEANT TO ROW TO THE
Temple? But I don't know anyone who lives
in the Temple!" Tony found it very little easier
to take in the next morning than he had in the middle of
the night. "Not only does it not make sense," he protested,
"but I have never in my life gone sleepwalking. Why
the devil should I take it up now? And a fool trick like
that! I might have drowned myself and not lived long
enough to know it."

Jo shivered. "Probably not so long as you stayed asleep.
But you'd have been bound to capsize if you'd wakened
out in mid-channel in the pitch dark. I suppose that's why
the police stopped trying to rouse your attention once they

guessed what the problem was. One of them had to wade in after the rowboat, but neither of them fancied the swim they would have had in the dark if you fell overboard."

Tony held his mug out for more coffee. "I must have gone to bed too tired and keyed up after all of yesterday's excitement. My shoulders and arms are stiff as blazes. Maybe I ought to take an hour or two off this afternoon in the tub with a good book. Soak the kinks out." He looked at his watch. "Did you root out the ABC to check on the trains? My rehearsal call is for ten-thirty, and if you mean to keep the car, you'll have to run me to the station."

"Right. I will need the car if I'm to see to the utilities and the roof and some kitchen equipment. So you have your choice of Brentford Junction in fifteen minutes or Isleworth in ... twenty-four."

On the way to Isleworth Station Jo said—too casually for an impulse of the moment—"Just a thought, Roger, but if you stayed up in town until after the Wednesday matinee too, you could make a start at packing up some of our things. And bring down some *clothes*. By Wednesday I shall hate the sight of an unironed denim shirt, clean or not! Besides," she added, "your hopeless father needs someone to do his breakfast for him."

It suited Roger well enough. "I don't mind." He grinned. "And if the old man tries another two-o'clock walk I'll be right on his heels. That is what you meant, isn't it?"

Tony directed an amused glance at him in the rear-view mirror. "How would you like to belt up?"

At Waterloo Station as they handed in their tickets to the guard at the platform gate, Tony asked suddenly,

"Care to see the play tonight? We may not be as up as we were last week, but at least my first act should be better. I got off to a dragging start on opening night—bad timing, the lot—but by Thursday it had come right. We can have supper somewhere afterward. Sound all right to you?"

"Gosh, yes." Roger had missed his father's opening night because of a Schools Orchestra concert in which he had played. "Don't they save the front seats to sell on the day of performance?"

"Yes. And *no*," Tony said firmly. "I do not care to catch a subliminal glimpse out of the corner of my eye of you sitting down there a-scowl with concentration. Moreover, as you well know, they are not the good seats. You want a feeling for the performance as a whole, not just a chance to see whose tights are wrinkled."

"I like to watch the faces." Roger objected mildly, though he knew from experience that it was useless.

From the station to the theatre was only a shortish walk. Tony and Roger parted at the head of the Upper Ground, Tony going round the parking-ramp corner to the stage entrance and Roger off to the "Today's Performance" box office. There was a queue—a mixed lot of tourists, old hands, and students—for returns and the cheaper seats reserved until the day of performance. Roger lounged around, re-reading the posters and looking through the brochures for the current and next booking periods. Next week, he noted idly, the *Hamlet* ran for five performances; the week after for only two.

It was a good ten minutes before the telephone message came through from Tony up in the dressing-rooms. The box-office supervisor beckoned to Roger.

"You're Roger Nicholas? Your father just rang down

about a seat for you, and we're in luck. We were holding a good single in the centre of Row H for someone who's just cancelled. I'll put it aside for you until tonight." He smiled. "To spare the feelings of the queue. Enjoy the play tonight."

"I will, thanks," said Roger, but he had a twinge of regret for Rows B or C in spite of Tony's insistence that actors played "over the heads" of the front rows.

On a sudden impulse, instead of walking up past the main box office and out, Roger took advantage of a moment when no one was looking in his direction to go quickly and quietly the other way. Moving up the carpeted stair, he kept to the shadows, and on the mezzanine level found himself in luck. The doors into the Circle of the Lyttelton Theatre should have been locked, but one had been overlooked. Easing one leaf of the door open, Roger slipped inside. The house lights were half up so he didn't dare try for a seat, but kept instead to the shadowed gangway.

On stage a thin young man was sweeping inside the thin lead circle that marked the central acting area on the dark floor. The set was simple, but imposing. Converging lead-coloured lines led from the forestage across the circle to a massive portal at the rear, an arrangement that could suggest either the interior or exterior of the Danish castle of Elsinore. A man wearing earphones appeared from behind the false proscenium to the right of the stage to announce, "Ready when you are," to a bearded man sitting at the centre of the stalls seats below.

"I've been ready for five minutes. Where's Tony?"

"Here," Tony called. He appeared at stage right in breeches and tights with his shirt half-buttoned and a doublet over his arm.

66

Tony and several of the others sat on the apron of the stage, and when everyone on call had gathered, the man in the stalls put aside his clipboard and notes and said, "Originally I called this rehearsal because Tony and I wanted to smooth a few things out, and I made it a costume call because we want to try a few changes in lighting intensity: one in this scene, and a few more complicated ones in the play-within-the-play. The changes we made to adapt to Tony's height and colouring still need some adjustment. However, it turns out that Rosencrantz has come down with the flu overnight and Andrew will be standing in, so we'll make it a full run-through of the Rosencrantz and Guildenstern scenes, and set the lighting changes when we come to them."

When the house lights had dimmed to a glow, the run-through began. To Roger, who had seen only a film of *Hamlet*, and that when he was too young to care for any of it but the ghost and the sword-fighting, it seemed to go smoothly enough. It was, in the way of many rehearsals, more a matter of movement and timing, of business and rhythms and inflections rather than the full deceptions and passions these would embody in an actual performance. When it came to Rosencrantz's news that the travelling players were come to Elsinore—the actors from the city that Hamlet had so enjoyed—Tony's Hamlet asked "Do they hold the same estimation they did when I was in the city? Are they so followed?"

The new Rosencrantz made a gesture of regret. "No indeed they are not."

And then the scene began to fall apart at the seams. Rosencrantz and Guildenstern stood dumbfounded as Hamlet answered with bitter humour, "It is not very strange. For my uncle is King of Denmark, and those that would make mouths at him while my father lived, give twenty, forty, fifty—a hundred ducats apiece—for his picture in little. S'Blood, there is something in this more than natural, if philosophy could find it out."

There was an awkward silence, broken by a half-hearted flourish of trumpets from offstage, before the man sitting in the stalls called, "For God's sake, Tony, don't you know what you did? You cut the whole of the little eyases."

Tony shaded his eyes to look out across the footlights. "I what?"

"The 'little eyases' passage. The child actors across the river." The voice rose with a faint edge to its patient tone. "Andy, give him the cue again. And Tony? Dress to your left about three feet. You're crowding. O.K. Andy?"

Rosencrantz repeated his gesture. "No indeed they are not."

Tony scowled. "How is that? No—How comes . . . it?" He sketched an angry flourish in the air. "All right, what is it? I would remind you that it's not two weeks since you cut the passage."

The director looked up from conferring with a second man wearing earphones who had come to sit beside him in the stalls. "*I* cut it? What are you on about?"

Tony's face sharpened and his voice grew tight and flat. "I happened to be speaking the scene as you instructed."

"The hell you were! Somebody give him a script."

In the Circle, Roger was unaccountably frightened. He eased erect from sitting on his heels and fell further back into the shadows. Even without stage makeup Tony, standing there in doublet, breeches, and tights, body all tension, his face darkened in confusion and frustration,

68

was a frightening echo of the man on the darkened landing. The illusion vanished as the house lights came up halfway, but there was still an uncomfortable feeling in the air as Tony, taking the script that was passed from the stage manager to Guildenstern to Rosencrantz, read through the passage, scanned it sharply once again, and tossed the script back to its owner in a long, neat arc.

"Very well," he said with obscure amusement. "Had I known that you did not mean after all to end the war, I would have been ready with the speech, as little as I like it. Shall we go on?"

The looks that were exchanged at this comment conveyed complete mystification, but when Tony gave Hamlet's "How comes it? Do they grow rusty?" Rosencrantz took the cue with a hasty "Nay, their endeavour keeps in the wonted pace; but there is, sir, an eyrie of children, little eyases, that cry out..." and the scene went on without a hitch. At its end Roger, not knowing just what it was that he had dreaded, slipped out to make his way downstairs and onto the Embankment.

At Hamilton Terrace Roger eased the tightness in his middle with a glass of milk and a lunch of yoghourt and tinned peaches, then packed his cello down to the bus stop, where he boarded a Number 8 bus for Tottenham Court Road and Professor Albert Clock's dark little flat off Museum Street.

At the end of his hour he had to tell the old man that the Nicholases were moving to Isleworth and that he would not be coming again. It was as much a struggle to get the words out as if he were cutting a last, frail mooring rope. For five years, not counting the one spent in

California, Professor Clock had been the single, sure, predictable thing in life: Thursdays at five during term time, Mondays and Thursdays at two during holidays. "Home" might shift endlessly, and schools follow each other in dreary succession, but the musty little flat with its floor awash in tumbled heaps of string solos and orchestral scores, and its faint, ever-present odour of cat-box, had always been there. This past year had been spent, Roger knew, in concealing the fact that there was really nothing more the old professor could teach him. The prospect of cutting loose, of finding another teacher who might be less reassuring, more demanding, more passionately (if not more completely) involved in music, had been too dismaying. But now the cord was cut.

Roger stepped off the bus at Elgin Avenue without the least recollection of having caught it in the first place, but feeling a little better about Albert Clock. It meant at least an end to pretending. All the way up the hill and along past St. Mark's Church he expected to find Tony at home—if not in the bath with the latest Michael Innes mystery, then out in the sunny garden. But he was not there.

Roger unlocked the door of the little coach house, propped the cello case in a corner of the entryway, and called; but Tony did not answer. There was no sign of him upstairs in the wide-windowed sitting room or in the garden below, so Roger retrieved the cello and went on through the passage to the bedrooms, which were in the basement of the large house adjoining. The coach house, before the conversion of the big house into flats, had once served as just that: a carriage-house and then garage.

He left the cello in his own room (or rather, Amy Dance's—he could not think of its rose and grey sleekness as his), and then checked Jo and Tony's room and the bathroom. Finding no sign that Tony had been home at all, he went through to the kitchen for another glass of milk, using sugar, an egg, orange juice and the blender to make it into a passable version of an Orange Julius, and took it in to watch a tennis match on the TV. Gradually, as one sharply contested game followed another, he forgot the vague, unnamed disquiet over his father. However unpredictable, Tony was quite able to look out for himself. Even when sunk in deepest gloom he could be counted on to come bobbing to the surface before long, with a cheerfulness to rival Alan's.

The tennis match was tied again, two sets all, when Roger decided to leave. There was nothing in the fridge to hold him until supper after the play, and he needed time to find something to eat on the way. On impulse he took from the lounge bookcase a battered paperbound copy of *Hamlet* and set out for the Maida Vale underground station. He took a train to Charing Cross, crossing the Thames by the footbridge to the Festival Hall, where he joined the queue in the cafeteria and chose two ham sandwiches, tea, ice cream, and chocolate cake and took them to a window table. As he ate he riffled through the pages of *Hamlet* in search of the scene he had seen played that morning.

It had been Act II, Scene 2, and he learned from the footnotes that the "little eyases"—the boy actors of the Children of the Chapel Royal and of St. Paul's—were not only worrisome competitors of the public playhouses, including Shakespeare's Globe Theatre, but added insult

71

to injury with satiric attacks on the adult players. But what all that might have to do with Tony's strange comment about disliking the speech remained obscure. At seven Roger closed the book with a defeated slap and set out to walk the short distance along the Embankment to the theatre.

The play was incredible. From the first appearance of the Ghost, Roger was caught by a sense of hurtling inertia, of unwilled movement toward catastrophe, and stunned by the power of the play even though he suspected some of it passed him by. Even the reflective moments when Tony was alone onstage were not still, but notes held and explored for a measure with no sense of easing in that inexorable movement. The pace slowed; the timing held. And the movement of the whole swept on. It never faltered, though there were moments when it seemed as if Tony somehow were the timekeeper even when he had no part in a scene—a conductor willing, cajoling, holding his musicians to a pitch and precision beyond what they willed themselves. His voice, compelling, with an odd, soft shadow of accent, his gestures—even the line of his back turned upon the audience—were the notes of a fine instrument played with intensity and ease, passion and restraint. Roger's private belief that his father was one of the best actors anywhere almost faltered. It seemed incredible that even Tony could be so good.

At the interval the audience sat stunned for fully half a minute before breaking into a groundswell of applause; and when at the final curtain Hamlet's body was borne away in honour at Fortinbras' command, Roger found his eyes were filled with tears. The applause was thunderous,

72

and went on for so long and for so many curtain calls even after the house lights came up, that it died away only when the iron safety curtain was closed in an unusual and unmistakable gesture of finality.

The crush at the exits was heavy, and by the time Roger emerged, a pale and exhausted Tony was already waiting out on the Embankment. Roger spotted him slouched under one of the dolphin lamps, trying to look anonymous.

"I made a run for it," Tony said with a shadow of a grin. "I couldn't face bein' trapped back at the stage entrance. Would you mind very much if we skipped that late supper and took a taxi directly home? I know I promised, but I'm not really up to it. I feel like an empty toothpaste tube."

Roger, still gripped by an unaccustomed awe, swallowed with difficulty. "Sure, Pa," he whispered.

Four hours later Roger was wakened from darkness and a shapeless dream into a guttering circle of light and the chill of a cold cloth on his forehead. A thin runnel of water slid past his ear and down his neck. The bed was his accustomed bed and the room Amy Dance's, but there was little comfort in the recognition.

A single candle burned in a brass candlestick on the bedside table, and a basin of water sat beside it. On a chair drawn up beside the bed, Tony sat, round-shouldered with exhaustion and his face streaked with tears. As Roger watched in bewilderment, his father wrung out the rag over the basin and reached out to replace it tenderly on his forehead.

"Ah, Jack. Dear Jack." Tony groaned and covered his

face with his hands. "Why must you've followed me back into this pesthole? 'Tis hard enough Kath'rine should leave me for a tinsel gallant. Now you'll have caught your death and I must lose you and Kitten both."

O there be players
that ʃI haue ʃeene play

TONY STILL HAD NOT STIRRED AT TEN, and Roger let him sleep. If he were supposed to be at the theatre someone would telephone soon enough, but Roger did not expect that. The engagement calendar in the kitchen showed nothing for the morning, only notes of an afternoon rehearsal, the evening performance, and the cryptic scribble *Coll.Th. P. gn f/Jo.* Collecting something for Jo?

Tony finally appeared a little before eleven, dressed, shaven, and looking relaxed and rested. The outfit made Roger, who rarely saw him in anything but jeans and denim shirts, blink. The blue velvet, silver-buttoned

Navajo shirt from Arizona and the pepper-coloured Italian slacks had only once before been off their clothes hangers, and that in California.

He said nothing about having had a restless night, and Roger, after an unhappy wrangle with himself, decided not to mention the strange, unhappy sleepwalking scene. Once fully awake himself, he had coaxed Tony back to his own bed and then wakened him. But if he remembered nothing of all that, why, let it lie, Roger thought gratefully. He could not have explained why it had frightened him so. Besides, if worry was at the root of sleepwalking, then the less of it Tony had, the better.

Roger went ahead of his father into the kitchen. "I'll do the breakfast. You read the newspaper." He turned on the grill to re-heat the already cooked sausages and switched on the electric kettle.

Tony moved to the place set for him at the table by the back window. "Am I meant to begin with the grapefruit or the *Guardian*? From your look of the cat that's been at the cream, I would guess the paper. On the Arts page?"

Roger nodded, and while he poured the boiling water into the coffee filter kept one eye on his father's spreading grin. The *Guardian*'s second-look review of last night's performance ought to be enough to set him up for weeks.

Marvelling, Tony lowered the paper and met Roger's eyes. "Was I really that good?"

Roger's grin matched his own. "Better," he said happily, easing two eggs into a pan of boiling water and setting the timer.

"If everyone says so, I suppose I must've been," Tony admitted with disarming candour. "A happy chance, too, havin' a critic in the house. He did a piece Saturday before last about my first performance, so this is pure gravy." He leaned back to read aloud, relishing every word: " 'In my enthusiasm for the original production I did not miss this quickened pace or the fluency and tension of ensemble playing which helped to make last night's performance so astonishing, but having been brought literally to the edge of my seat, I may never again be content to sit well back and accept a pleasing sum of unequal parts as a whole.' Hah! There's praise indeed!"

Everything was back to normal, Roger thought. He really ought to watch himself, imagining heaven knows what, spinning terrors out of worry and wild dreams. There was nothing out of the way in Tony's being erratic and unpredictable. Who should know that better than Roger? Last night's sleepwalking, and Sunday's, were just a new wrinkle in opening-weeks nerves. Tony invested a tremendous amount of emotional energy in a new role—or as in the case of *Hamlet*, re-thinking a familiar one—and until that expense of effort stretched it, like a new glove being shaped to his hand, he always *had* required a bit of nursemaiding. *And devil take him, have I not given it? What need has he of Katherine? I would be glad of a way to wring dear Kitten's neck!*

The words slid into Roger's mind as he poured away the water and spooned the eggs from the pan: a deep-thrust pinprick of sound that did not even register at first but bloomed in the next moment into panic. The dish shattered in the sink, eggshell, yolk and shards all mixed together.

"Problems?"

"No." Roger turned his back to the table. "Not if you

don't mind having just the one egg," he managed. "I've made a mess of the other one."

"Oh, one's enough when I have breakfasted on praise," Tony declaimed irrepressibly. "Besides, there's toast enough for three."

"I'll do you another in a minute," Roger mumbled, not hearing. He pushed the egg cup on its plate in front of his father and turned away. Moving carefully, as if the floor itself were paved with eggshells, he went out into the passage and closed the door quietly behind him. For a moment he thought he would be sick, but the worst of the feeling passed and he made his way to the pink-and-grey bedroom to throw himself face downward on the bed. When the trembling stopped, he turned over and stared at the roses on the ceiling. What had happened? It had been like hearing a ham radio operator's broadcast drift across the Radio 3 wavelength—a phrase or two, then nothing. There was no understanding the bitter words that had unfolded in his mind like an opening seed. A bitter almond seed. Some mad little trick of the mind. And yet....

And yet it was his father who had given Kitten her name. Last night. Last night Roger had decided that Katherine had to be Cathy—Cathy Rockford—who, when she and Tony had split up three years ago, had gone off to Italy and married a rich vineyard owner. But Roger had liked her. He had certainly never wanted to throttle her. Kitten. *Puss* ... No! What he had to put out of his mind was that it had anything to do with the old house in Isleworth. That was craziness. Even if an old house really could be haunted by a long-dead tragedy, *this* house had no Tudor bones inside its heavy Edwardian walls. And the National Theatre was new from the ground up. It *was*

Cathy Rockford Tony had moaned over. Not that that was a cheerful thought either.... And Jack? Well, it was easy enough to get Jack out of Roger John Nicholas. Perhaps he'd been called Jack when he was small. The rest of what his father had said—his mind shied away from that. The rest of it was just muddle. This morning had to be more of the same: his own tired muddle.

Roger sat up on the edge of the bed feeling much better. His stomach still fluttered, but that would stop. Roger John Nicholas, pathological worrier! He really would have to watch that. Even justifiable worries solved themselves nine times out of ten if you didn't pick and prod, but ignored them.

Determined to be cheered, Roger went out and shakily put another egg to boil.

There was a two-thirty call for a second reading of *Moondoggle*, a new play due to open in October, and Roger decided to tag along with Tony to the theatre. No reason, he told himself. He just felt like it. To his surprise, Tony took his second taxi in twenty-four hours, hailing one at the Maida Vale crossing instead of carrying on to the underground station. In it they detoured by way of a shop just off Bond Street where Tony picked up an elegantly-wrapped parcel, and they disembarked at the theatre stairs on the south end of Waterloo Bridge with an extravagant tip to the driver. Tony made the rehearsal on time, but with only minutes to spare.

Rehearsal rooms were off-limits—and had no conveniently obscure doors and gangways—so Roger found himself a sunny spot on one of the terraces and settled down to devour the last part of the mystery he had begun while Tony slept the morning away. Once it was finished,

79

he took up practising the cello in his head, sitting on the base of a massive sculpture with his knees just so, the bowing and fingering precise, his eyes almost closed in a deep and pleasurable concentration.

Alan Collet found him there at four o'clock, the invisible bow poised, then darting into a last complex and moving passage. "Bravo!" He applauded as Roger lowered the imaginary bow. "What was that?"

"Bach's G major solo cello suite. The final gigue," Roger said. He sighed. "Casals played one of the suites every day from the time he was thirteen, so I thought I would too, but last week I gave up and started counting the ones I play without the cello. What I need is a cello that folds up to briefcase size. Where's Pa? I thought you would be another hour."

"He will be. I just died at the end of the first act."

"What's it about? And who are you?"

"I, I am told, am highly significant. I'm an astronaut named MacDool and your father, if you will believe it, is Ossip Korngold, a Cambridge radio astronomer. As for what it may be about, ask me at Christmas." He rolled the script into a fat tube and inspected a barge on the river. "At first blink it sounds like a cross between *Space 1999* and a sendup of *Being and Time*—deep Cherman philozophy," he explained in a thick German accent. "You will think it exceedingly funny even if you don't understand half of what goes on. *I* think it exceedingly funny and hope to understand the first act by the time we open."

Lowering the makeshift telescope, Alan cast a sideways look at Roger. "I hear I missed the performance of the year last night. How did old Tony come out of it?"

Roger flashed him the Nicholas grin. " 'Like an empty

toothpaste tube,' he said. He slept almost until noon."

"You were there, I take it?" Alan was, for Alan, oddly sober. "I may come in tonight myself. Care to join me? It means standing, to judge by that queue down below."

"I don't mind that," Roger said hastily. He had half meant to come anyway.

Alan sat down with his back to the parapet and looked at Roger consideringly. "Queer thing happened yesterday. I came by to pick up this script and found your old man standing in the middle of his dressing room in a complete fog. He seemed to snap out of it after a minute or so and asked if I wanted to go out for a bite of lunch at the Cardinal's Hat."

"So?" Roger wondered at Alan's puzzled tone.

"There's no such place. He led off down the Upper Ground and then got himself all turned round down by Blackfriars Road. I finally twigged that what he was after was supposed to be on Bankside—some new place down by Cardinal Cap Alley, I supposed—so I steered us under the railway bridge and up Hopton Street. And that's when he said the damnedest thing. He said 'This is the first time I've come on Green Walk across the fields. We're like to have the dogs set on us before we find a place to cross the ditch.' Almost knocked me sideways, that did."

"It might be out of a play," Roger suggested.

"No. It wasn't the old quotation lark." Alan frowned unhappily. "There was an odd, uncertain quirk to it, and I think he meant it. He had to be a million miles away. When we turned onto Bankside it was as if he had never in his life seen the gravel works and the power station, when they're as ugly as Hades and not what I would call forgettable. Anyhow, when we came to Cardinal Cap

Alley, old Tony was looking for his pub and it wasn't there. There were the same mildly pleasant old houses as always, nothing else, and your dad looking like a baffled sleepwalker. I managed to get him down to the Anchor at the far end, and we took our lunch out onto the river wall. He wouldn't—or couldn't—say why he was so shaken; just ate, drank off his white wine, and came back here and slept for the rest of the afternoon. *Then* apparently he ups and gives the performance of his life." Alan turned on Roger a worried scowl. "What is it? He was feeling a bit off-colour on Sunday too."

Roger turned to lean on the parapet and look out over the river. "I don't know. Nerves, maybe. You said 'like a sleepwalker'," he added reluctantly. "Well, Pa's been doing that too. The last two nights. He says it's never happened before, so it must be the play that has him all nervy. I think this one matters more to him than anything else has."

"Of course it does, but galloping nerves don't seem old Tony's style," Alan said doubtfully. "I suppose it is possible. He ought to ease off a bit. The backstage reaction to last night's smash performance wasn't exactly Universal Love. I understand that he was making moves that threw some of the others off, made them really stretch—changing line readings, speeding up the pace, what-have-you. *Not* the sort of tricks to endear one to a director even when it does come off. To quote Andy Barron, 'This may not be *Godot*, but it's not the bloody last lap of the Indy 500 either.'"

"He won't do it tonight," Roger said defensively. "He feels great today. He's so *un*-up-tight he's almost unstrung."

"So I noticed. Peacocking it a bit, isn't he?" Alan's

frown cleared and he grinned. "Newspaper reviews over-flowing with superlatives do work great cures."

Tuesday evening's *Hamlet*, sold out down to the last of the standing-room, may not have matched Monday's in its pitch of feeling and tension but that was at least in part because the audience—and the cast—came fore-warned. The performance was deeply moving and Tony superb, but it was not the triumph of the previous night. Even so, it widened Alan's eyes. Fond as he was of Tony Nicholas, he would not have rated him as an actor as any more than very highly skilled. This Hamlet was that, yes, but far more. The softened colloquial accent startled him at first, but he came to hear how uncannily it fitted itself to the poetry. To Roger's repeated question of "What did you think of it?" he finally shrugged helplessly and said, "That has to be what Brook meant when he coined the term 'the Holy Theatre.' It is that."

Roger himself had enjoyed it thoroughly even though standing for so long gave him a cramp in one leg; and when he was wholeheartedly included in a large, im-promptu, late-supper expedition to Fulham, he began to wonder why he had never thought he might become an actor. Tony was in great form and spent one hilarious half hour teaching everyone a raucous word-game he called Tickle-brain; and when the party was winding down he borrowed a guitar to accompany himself in Dowland's gravely lovely old song, "I saw my lady weep." Roger had not even known he played the guitar and listened with awe and pleasure. It was a perfect evening.

Still, by the time he hit St. John's Wood and bed, Roger had come to the reluctant conclusion that he preferred less talk and more sleep. He would have to stick to the cello. Kicking off his shoes, he flopped onto the bed in all his clothes and was out almost as his head touched the pillow.

There had been nothing to worry about at all. Nothing at all.

Ile goe no further

OGER COULD NOT REMEMBER HAV-
ing got up again, and yet he must have, for
he sat in the big flowered armchair in the
high-windowed sitting room and dreamt. Or dreamt he
sat there. He was not sure which even though the heavy
linen was smooth under his hand, and, outside, the dark,
familiar lawn bordered by darker walls stretched from
the low sill at his knees to the shadowed trees at its end.
The trees were black against the street lamp beyond and
the pale, warm loom of city sky that hung like a glowing
border on the night.

The sound brought him erect in the chair: a click of the Yale lock on the garden door in the downstairs entry passage. Through the wide window he watched, frozen, and saw Tony, still fully dressed, emerge onto the lawn below to stand and look about him in bewilderment. His face was a blur against the darkness, indecipherable, but the bewilderment was easy to read. His movements were the uncertain starts and turns of a man who does not know where he is, who has taken the wrong turning and cannot decide where he took it. He did move at last, and it was Roger's turn to be bewildered, for Tony strode with sudden purpose towards the darkness under the trees.

Roger rose from the chair unwillingly. His mind pulled and coaxed like an anxious terrier trying to stir its sluggish master out for a walk. Stumbling down the stair, he fumbled the lock open and stepped out into the cool summer night. But he came to the trees too late. There was neither sound nor sign of his father. And nowhere he could have gone. The path curved through the trees and out again onto the lawn, but path and lawn were empty. There was a faint sound—the tap of heels on pavement—but it came from the little neighborhood park on the other side of the high garden wall, slow at first, then more sure, more rapid.

Climbing first onto the frame of the compost bin, Roger gained the roof of the garden shed and peered over the top of the wall down into the park. In the light from the street lamp the roundabout and swings and benches had a bleached, desolate look, as if the shrieking children were gone forever. For a moment it seemed almost—not quite, for he could not really see it—but almost as if a tree grew up through the centre of the

86

roundabout. Almost as if beyond the tree whose branches sheltered the shed roof where he crouched, a wide wood spread: a wood of great, broad trees with moonlight spilling through their branches.

But of course there was no moon to be seen in the cloudy sky. And the park was its old, familiar self. Roger heard the click of footsteps on the pavement again, beyond the gate, receding south along Violet Hill. It had to be Tony. Where else could he have gone? Stepping from the flimsy shed roof to straddle the wall, he worked round until he had a good grip, and dropped to the grass below. Once out over the park's low gate and across the street, he slowed. Tony had stopped at the corner of Abercorn Place and stood looking back, but seemed not to see him. For a moment Roger faltered, suddenly unsure whether it was Tony or only someone strangely like him. In the moment that he hesitated, the street lamp dimmed. Its yellowish glare bleached into a wash of moonlight, and along the street, the Abbey Tavern, the shopfronts, and the boxy block of flats were only pale shadows glimmering among trees. The footpath where he stood grew soft with leaf-mold, and a rutted cart-track angled down the middle of the car-lined street. The man some forty yards ahead who stood debating about his way for a moment both was and was not his father. By the clothes, as blurred as the landscape, it was and was not—equally—the man he had seen in the dark house in Isleworth.

Panic-stricken, Roger retreated the way he had come. When his hand closed round a bar of the iron park gate, he clutched it as if it were a life-preserver and he adrift beyond Gravesend, until his knuckles ached with the holding and the illusion of forest faded.

But he could not turn back home again. He ran, and as he ran he knew or felt that that other place had closed in behind him—that as the pub and the newsagent's flicked past the corner of his eye, trees grew up through them and the moonlight put out the street lamp. But he would not look. He refused to see. It was a trick, an old trick of dreams. All his five senses and his pounding heart insisted that he was awake, but it could only be a dream—vivid, lucid, but a dream. Even at that, he felt a panicky dread that it was a dream he could drown in.

Before the corner he slowed, unsure whether to try to stop Tony or simply to follow him as he crossed the road in the middle of the intersection and headed into Nugent Terrace. But as he wavered, one foot in the street, his father's shadowy figure angled up onto the pavement—and three yards further on disappeared through the wall of the shoe-repair shop.

Roger froze where he stood. *Through the wall of the shop. Through the wall.* . . . In a daze, Roger made his way across to it. Touched it. Ran his hands over the rough brick. It was inescapably solid, and yet he had seen what he had seen. He thrust his hands into his jeans pockets and drew back, confused and terribly afraid. He had promised to follow, but how could he? *I promised Jo,* he thought numbly. But he backed helplessly toward the corner.

As he stood there, staring at the wall, the other place—*the same place*—slipped silently past his guard and almost swallowed him into its other time. Against the moonlit wood of broad-limbed walnut trees there was only a pale shadow of the brick and the small paned windows where the building had been. The track cutting through the wood ran on, not quite straight, following like an eerie echo the long, fading line of a high brick wall that could only be the long wall forming the backs of the gardens down along Hamilton Terrace. Roger stood unbelieving, watching the past place engulf the present, rendering it as insubstantial as a scene glimpsed through fog: not gone, but unreal, a distant world smothered in silence.

The tall figure Roger had pursued was almost out of sight a hundred yards ahead. Torn between the urge to follow whether the cloaked, hatted figure were Tony or not, and terror at the nightmare thought that once on the path there would be no getting off it, he felt a sharp pain in one palm, and found himself clutching a seven-sided coin as fiercely as if it were a talisman against the past. 50 NEW PENCE, he knew it read. D·G·REG·F·D·1976 · ELIZABETH·II. 1976, not 1603. Elizabeth the Second, not the First. And whether it was the coin or the fear of that first step through the ghost of the little shoe-repair shop, the pavement grew firm under his feet and the red telephone kiosk loomed up reassuringly at his back.

For so long as he held fast. No more. He might stand on a corner of a tree-lined street, but the long-ago wood slept moon-silvered in the church and houses, among the horse-chestnuts, in the red kiosk, waiting. You *promised*, one part of him mourned, and another whispered in a far corner of his mind, *What can it be but the road from Kylbourne and the old Priory? He'll soon be past Punker's Barn and footing it apace, for the road down through the fields to Lillestone village is faster going, don't forget.*

Roger shut it out. He knew nothing of priories or barns. But Jo. . . . Without a thought for what he meant to do, he sprinted for the corner of Hamilton Terrace and turned south, paralleling the way the old track went. At Hall Road he knew he must still be well behind. There, the garden wall the old way followed came out along the mews entrance to a foreign-car sales and service garage, but across Hall Road there was no longer a through-way, only flats and houses and garden walls. So he kept straight on.

Hamilton Terrace ended at St. John's Wood Road, where Roger instinctively turned down towards the main road instead of taking the way past Lord's in towards the City and the Temple. On Sunday night Tony had meant to go by water to the Temple. What might be there besides the lawyers' lodgings and Blackfriars Bridge further along the Embankment, Roger was not sure. He strode on doggedly until a fleeting glimpse of a tall figure far ahead spurred him again into a jogging run past the sleeping reach of the Regent's Canal.

There the trees lining Maida Vale gave way to the first wide stretch of Edgeware Road, running down through a jumble of shops and flats towards Marble Arch. How was he to follow a half-seen shadow down that long and lamp-lit way—a wraith that he could not be sure was any more than a shadow in his mind's eye? If he got as far as the police section house by the Marylebone overpass without being noticed by a curious policeman, he could not hope to get much further. It was hopeless. There was a part of him—a part he feared—that recognized the old way in the new, that knew the road past Lillestone Manor and Paddington village came at last to Tyburn and the road east to St. Giles and London's City, but he shut his heart and mind against it. Tony had put a name to that part of him: Jack. And because he was afraid of Jack, who knew the way, he faltered, slowed, and stood lost in the long, still street.

Somewhere in the house there had been a noise. Roger woke, trembling, to find himself crouched knees-to-chest on his own bed. The first faint wash of morning showed grey through the window opening onto the front areaway. His shoes lay on the floor, but he was fully dressed and could not remember why. Last night? Last night he had been—where? Slowly, muzzily, it came back: at the theatre with Alan, then a huge spread of make-your-own sandwiches at someone's house. There had been talk and games and singing, and he had kept dropping off to sleep. Had slept most of the way home in the taxi. Remembering, he uncurled luxuriously from his tight, cramped knot and slid into a deep, dreamless sleep.

Awakening again at nine, what Roger remembered was his promise to Jo about the clothes. After a hasty breakfast he brought out two suitcases from the cupboard under the sitting room stairs and set about packing some of Pippa's things, and his own, and a few books. Jo's and Tony's could wait until he had made Tony a breakfast that would do for lunch as well since he liked to be at the theatre by noon on matinee days.

At ten Roger went in to wake Tony, feeling his way across the dark room to draw the heavy curtains and let the sun spill in. They whispered open, and when he turned again he saw his father stretched across the bed as if he had fallen there, his arms out-flung and sandalled feet dirtying the rumpled bedspread. Roger wanted to turn away and could not. He could only stare like a cornered woods-creature. Tony's feet were filthy, his velvet shirt

91

muddied. An ugly, swelling redness ran from above his temple down to his jaw.

And a scrap of bloody rag was knotted clumsily around his left hand.

These are but wilde and whurling words

TONY LOOKED ON WITHOUT MUCH interest as Roger swabbed the shallow gashes across his palm with antiseptic. "I don't know," he said. "I must've grabbed at somethin' sharp as I fell. It doesn't matter."

Alan Collet looked at Tony, sitting on the edge of the rumpled bed, with baffled concern. "What is that supposed to mean? I come by with an offer of transport for the gear Jo says young Roger here has been packing, find one half-packed case, you looking as if you had gone a round with Ali, and 'It doesn't matter'? That hand looks as if you had taken hold of a double-edged knife."

93

"I thought I had," Tony said indistinctly. "But there wasn't one."

"What did happen? Surely there has to be more to it than 'I must've been sleepwalkin' again.' Not, I grant you, that there aren't streets up yonder in Kilburn where you could manage to get yourself roughed up at two or three in the morning."

"Not Kilburn." Tony winced as he straightened the hand for the bandage Roger held ready. "I dreamt—I dreamt I had to go to Fleet Street to ask the porter at the Temple if he knew where Cliffe had gone, where in Essex it was he lived. I thought . . . it seemed I was set upon. Someone from out a dark doorway, I thought. But when I came round, a police constable was helping me up, and he said there'd been no one, that he'd seen me fall. It took a while convincin' him that I was capable, but in the end he saw me onto an N94 bus and told the conductor to make sure I didn't miss the Elgin Avenue stop. And here I am."

The question "Who is Cliffe?" sprang to Roger's tongue, but he bit it back. It didn't matter. It could not matter. His father had been walking in a dream. And seemed half in it still. Even his speech was strange—not softened, exactly, but . . . there were the elisions, the dropped Gs . . .

"Yes, here you are," Alan agreed worriedly, his grin more rueful than amused. "And look at you. You'll need an icebag for that swelling or you'll be a very lumpy Dane this afternoon indeed. Have you such a thing?"

"In the bathroom." Roger fixed the last strip of elastic tape round his father's hand. "I'll get it."

When he had disappeared, Alan asked, "What ails

young Roger? He seems as jumpy as a flea on a griddle. Is there something you've not told me?"

Tony shook his head wearily. "No, nothing. But you know kids. Give them somethin' they can't handle and they back away like wild animals. No look-ee, no wor-ry. I reckon he thinks the old man is fallin' apart and it frightens him. I must say I don't care for it much myself. I suppose I can thribble through this afternoon..." His voice trailed off uncertainly. "If only I could discover where Cliffe had gone," he whispered.

"Cliffe? You mentioned him before. Who is this Cliffe?"

Tony passed his good hand over his face as if that could clear away the cobwebs of his mind. "I...I don't know," he said muzzily. "But I think that when I find him I must kill him. Does that sound mad? I suppose it does."

Alan stared. "It certainly does," he said at last, as steadily as he could manage. "You are going to have to see a doctor, my friend."

"I suppose I am," Tony agreed slowly. "Jo knows one who—" He broke off as Roger came through from the kitchen with a bowl of ice and the ice bag.

"Jo knows one what?" Roger asked.

"Knows we're comin' down after the matinee," his father amended, making an effort to concentrate. "But if Alan's goin' to run our cases down we won't have to go through the rig'marole of puttin' them in the Left Luggage at Waterloo for the afternoon. We might send a box of books or two as well." He frowned. "When did Jo phone you about the things to go down, Alan?"

"Not Jo. Jemima."

Roger was startled. "Jemmy? But she went back to Cambridge."

Alan's eyes twinkled briefly. "She's not there now. Not with a lovely puzzle to poke and pry at in Isleworth. It seems that yesterday morning the itch grew so painful that she persuaded her boss to let her begin her holiday a week early, cleared her desk, and was in Isleworth in time to walk in on Jo and Pippa at teatime. She rang about an hour ago to tell me."

"That's great!" Roger exclaimed.

"Probably wants to make sure we don't wreck more than we restore," Tony observed with a glint of humour. "What had she uncovered this mornin'? A servants' loft up in the rafters?"

Alan looked at him searchingly, as if he were puzzled by something he could not quite put his finger on. "Nothing. At least not in the house. Seems Jo put your solicitors onto tracing the property title back through the legal records, and then paid a call on the rector to find out whether there might be anything in the old parish registers."

"Do they go back that far?" Roger asked eagerly. "What did she find?"

"Oh, they go back," Alan said, almost evasively. "To 1566. It seems there was one entry among the burials that might give a lead to your original householder—something about 'New House, by the parsonage.' Jo's back at it today, trying to see if she can find some other trace. Since the fire in the old church, the registers have been kept in Hounslow Public Library, so she's there and Jemmy's across at Syon House trying to charm her way into the manuscript collection to check through their early seventeenth-century local maps and plans. Pippa and the animals are holding down the fort."

"All very industrious, aren't they? And here I sit playin' *prima donna*." Grimacing, Tony pushed himself erect and took the filled ice bag from Roger. "I can at least look through the closet and drawers in here and see what needs packin', and then you can look out a box or two for the books. There's that parcel I picked up yesterday, too. Mustn't forget that."

Alan moved to the bedroom doorway. "I wouldn't bother about the books," he said with an almost convincing show of now-how-did-I-manage-to-miss-the-obvious. "There won't be room. I haven't anything on for this afternoon but an errand or two, so it makes better sense to do them first and run you two *and* the cases down after the matinee."

"In rush-hour traffic? You can't," Tony objected. "You're playin' tonight."

"I'm not on until the middle of the second act. And we can make good time going out Wandsworth way to Upper Richmond Road and then across Twickenham Bridge instead of through the West End. Isleworth isn't the end of the earth. I'll be back in good time."

Tony, moving after him into the hallway, paused, his face in shadow. "It has proved th'end of my earth," he murmured.

Alan looked quickly from Tony to Roger but Roger, his face set and calm, moved on, apparently not having heard. "Right, then," Alan said with a passable imitation of his usual good cheer. "Why don't I conjure up three of the famous Collet omelettes while you two are at your packing. I can't leave the cases in the open car all after-

97

noon, so I'll drop you and them off at the theatre. O.K.?"

Tony gave him a wry smile. "Gen'rous of you. And welcome to the nursemaid brigade."

After dropping Tony and Roger at the theatre Alan turned the MG north again across Waterloo Bridge, then up Aldwych and Kingsway. He felt a bit uneasy about not sticking to Tony for the afternoon since Roger seemed determined to see nothing odd in his father's behavior. As for the *Hamlet*, Tony's understudy had been alerted—discreetly and just in case—so there was nothing more to be done but hope for the best. As he drove, Alan tried to pin down just what sort of crazy bee it was that he had in his bonnet.

Tony was clearly in trouble. Of course it might be some private, personal complication and none of his business, but Alan's instincts said no. The tale Jemima had poured out over the telephone of Pippa's ghost and the "wall" across the bedroom doorway must have started him off. When you added young Roger's divination of the old staircase and his more than usually tight and nervous manner—the familiar act of nonchalance had worn pain-fully thin—it began to sound suspiciously as if the old house really were haunted. Idiotic thought, but there it was. Tony's sleepwalking had begun in Isleworth. Even more disquieting, to Alan's way of thinking, were his odd, waking lapses: that search for a non-existent tavern, the uncomfortable rehearsal scene Andy Barron had re-counted, and those two astonishing performances that combined Tony's considerable best with something more formal and vibrant, more disciplined, more alive to the verse as poetry.

Alan scowled at the red traffic light by Kingsway Underground Station. Tony was simply not that brilliant. Yet Monday night's performance, if it really had topped last night's, must have been transcendent. "Transcendent." Frightening word when you came right down to it: a performance that took the best of two worlds and made of it something incredible. The best of two worlds... that was the bee in his bonnet. That faint touch of accent the *Guardian* critic had commented on had come and gone yesterday afternoon, and had been even stronger in last night's performance. If it had not seemed obtrusive then, it was because it was consistent and seemed an oddly right and natural part of the blank verse. But this morning? Turning into Great Russell Street, Alan made for the Bloomsbury Square underground parking. Finding an empty place on the street could take a good half hour, and the five-minute walk to the University Library in Senate House was a lot less wearing. No, he thought. This morning that pleasant, softened accent had been distinctly unnerving. An echo of the past.

On the fourth floor of Senate House, Alan flashed his out-of-date reader's ticket and breezed past the porter and through the turnstile as if he were still a member of the university with a perfect right to be there. He had taken his English lit degree five years before, but was in and out often enough that the porters on regular duty always remembered him with a friendly nod. Without a current ticket he could not take out books, but it was possible to do some good, uninterrupted reading at one of the tables down among the open shelves. On the second level he found the section he was looking for and collected an armload of books to take to the vacant table by the nearest window: Andrew Gurr's *The Shakespearean Stage 1574–1642*, Baldwin's *The Organisation and Personnel of the Shakespearean Company*, M. C. Bradbrook's *The Rise of the Common Player*, T. L. Irons' two volumes, *The King's Men at the Globe* and *The Queen's Children at Blackfriars*, F. E. Halliday's *Shakespeare in His Age*, and Kökeritz's *Shakespeare's Pronunciation*. A good afternoon's-worth of skimming. Choosing a volume at random, he leafed through to the index pages.

And found what he was looking for.

On the whole the matinee performance went well enough, but Roger, standing at the rear of the auditorium, found himself increasingly bothered by having to listen so hard. The accent Tony had been using so effectively seemed to have become an obsession. In the final scenes it sounded almost an affectation—a cross between Lord Peter Wimsey's fashionably-dropped Gs and the flattened vowels of—of Boston, Massachusetts. The contrast with the other members of the cast began to be marked, though they gallantly followed his lead far enough to soften the effect. The worst moment, however, had come during the Rosencrantz and Guildenstern scenes when twice Tony appropriated lines that belonged to Guildenstern and then drifted into a confusion that a brilliant job of covering by the other actors could barely mask.

After the final curtain Roger's distress was eased a little by overhearing a smartly-dressed woman say to a friend, "We really would have done better to queue for the evening performance. Matinees do have a way of being rather slapdash." Which was true often enough. Tony said as much himself. Matinee audiences often were less knowledgeable and less responsive, so the temptation was always there to let down, to ease off.

But it was harder for Roger to deceive himself when the porter at the stage door sent him along to the second dressing-room level to give Alan a hand with Tony and their cases. Alan, cold-creaming off the last of Tony's stage makeup, said only, "Fetch us a glass of water and a couple of aspirins, will you, Rog? Your dad has a fierce thirst and a fiercer headache. I think the sooner we get him home to Jo the better. Looks to me like the flu coming on."

Roger moved numbly to the sink and came back to offer the glass and pills in silence, for the red-rimmed eyes that had met his in the dressing-room mirror might have been a stranger's. Tony looked more than exhausted: blank, utterly drained.

"S'all right," he said vaguely. "Only a touch of th'ague. It'll pass." But he was short of breath and when he rose, saying "Han' me the shirt there on th' chair," his outstretched hand shook.

The trip down to Isleworth, with the cases strapped on the luggage rack and Roger crammed sideways in the jump seat along with the precious parcel for Jo, was made in silence. Tony felt too rotten for conversation, and no one else cared to say a word. They pulled up in front of the house just before seven and Alan, after a kiss and a hastily carved chicken leg presented by Jemima, was on his way back to town five minutes later, leaving his afternoon's notes in her hand. "I'll be back by midnight," he promised.

Jemima had been startled. "I didn't know *you* meant to join the house party. What's up?"

"That's up." Alan flicked a finger at the pocket note-book in her hand. "Have a look at it after Jo's tucked Tony in for the night. And keep an eye on young Roger's reaction. There's something queer going on, and I have a feeling he's part of it."

I could a tale vnfolde

THE DRESS HUNG ON ONE OF THE open French doors, fluttering against the green evening like a gorgeous beribboned chiffon butterfly, green and gold, lemon and rose. Jo's astonished pleasure—shock, even—had roused Tony from his lethargy enough to make him refuse the offer of a brand-new bed and insist on sitting down to dinner. Every time Jo's eyes strayed to the lovely gown, Tony's were on her as hungrily as if he had not seen her in weeks. It was not a comfortable meal.

"Dinner's wonderful, Jo," Roger said to break the silence. He attacked a second piece of chicken with enthusiasm. "And the house looks halfway human." The table was still the yellow door, but now it was supported at a sensible height on two carpenters' saw horses and covered with a blue and white Welsh linen cloth. They sat on handsome ash folding chairs. Even the bare front room with its four canvas lawn chairs had been given a touch of elegance by a large white paper globe glowing like a soft moon in the centre of the ceiling where an ornately ugly fixture had hung before. And there were beds—so far only mattresses and box-springs set on wheeled frames, but *beds*. "How did you do so much if you were off poking around churches and libraries?"

Jo raised an eyebrow. "Inspiration, my dear. I had a brainstorm after I saw you two off and went along to the hardware shop to buy a light bulb for a belated experiment. It turned out that the electricity had been on all the while. The lights were either burned-out or had no bulbs at all. The water's not having been shut off should have made us suspicious that dear Aunt Deb's protégés had left us their electric bill as well, but when none of the lights worked, I never gave it a second thought. Anyway, after I switched on the hot water heater, Pippa and I waltzed out to buy a second-hand electric cooker. We settled on an oversized beauty that is now installed in absurd spendour in that shambles of a kitchen downstairs. The beds and lampshades and linens were simple. I rang Heals, and they made this morning's delivery."

"I got to sign for them," said Pippa with satisfaction, "and showed where everything was supposed to go. Then I made the beds."

Tony left off toying with his chicken and smiled faintly at that. "A good thing, too, sweetheart." He sighed. "I think bed's where I should be after all. Might as well give up tryin' to fight it. Sorry to be the spectre at the feast, but Jemim'll forgive me, won't you love?" He scraped his chair back unsteadily.

"Of course, Tony." Jemima's earnest blue eyes followed his progress down the steps into the front room. When he was out of earshot she rose purposefully. "I'm going down to the Apprentice for a little bottle of cognac, Jo. That's flu all right. Once it's laid him flat he'll not be able to keep anything down, but a teaspoonful in a glass of hot water helps to see you through that. It's an old jungle remedy my missionary granny taught me."

"I wonder if there's anything Jemima doesn't have an answer for," Jo murmured as she excused herself in turn. "I'd better go up to be sure Tony's all right. You two can clear the plates, if you will. There's some fancy cheese downstairs on the kitchen table if you'd like something more than fruit for dessert." She drifted down into the front room quite calmly, but a moment later her quiet footsteps could be heard taking the stairs two steps at a time.

Roger fumbled at his second orange, pulling off the peel in ragged patches. "So, Pips," he said nervously, wrenching his mind away from the comings and goings upstairs. "If Jo and Jemmy were poking around in a lot of musty old books and papers, what did they turn up? Alan said something about a 'New House.' In a burial record? *Was* this house the one?"

"I guess so. They were awfully excited," Pippa said. "They didn't explain what was so special, though. I think it's supposed to be a secret from Tony, because they said if Alan found out anything it would make the best birthday surprise ever."

Roger looked at her blankly. "But his birthday was in January."

"When I had the measles, remember? And the birthday party got called off. Well, they were laughing about having a surprise party instead of a housewarming. This Sunday, maybe. A big picnic for a zillion people to celebrate the house and Tony's play and everything."

Roger was uneasy. "What did Jo find to get them that steamed-up?" He reached across to Jemima's vacant place to pick up Alan's dog-eared notebook and flip through the pages.

"It's here somewhere." Pippa slipped from her chair and crossed to the old staircase. A length of clothesline had been looped across to close it until the upper railings were back in place, but the lower steps had been scraped and washed clean of the long years' grime and put to use as temporary shelving for a toolbox, cleaning materials, and a stack of papers and library books. From one of the books Pippa drew a thin sheaf of notes paper-clipped together, and pulled loose the top sheet to bring and place in front of Roger.

Roger laid Alan's notebook open face down on the table, picked up the slip of paper, and read the first entry twice over before its significance leapt out at him:

1603 Eureka! Parts illegible because of damage at time of fire, but the following appears under

26^t December *Buried in the church with a knell of III for the monthes of his lyf, Christopher, infant son of Thomas Garland, pl...r and Katherine, of New House b......rsonidge.*

106

Could "pl. . .r" by some wild, wonderful freak be *player*? Thomas Garland rings a bell somewhere. And the blank-blank-rsonidge is obviously "by the parsonage." Could this have been north of the church instead of west where the present rectory is?

"Can you tell what all the fuss was about?" Pippa paused in tossing grapes to Sammy to ask, "What could he have played *at* that was so great?"

"Not games," Roger said numbly. "They called actors 'players'."

"Honestly?" Pippa was delighted. "Like Tony! That would be the excitingest unbirthday surprise ever, wouldn't it? Do you suppose Katherine was an actress like Mama? I'll bet she was."

"There weren't actresses back then," Roger said distantly. He reached once more for the spiral notebook. "I suppose they thought it would be immoral somehow. Anyway, boys always played the women's parts."

"*Boys?*" Pippa was astonished. "I'll bet *they* felt silly."

But Roger scarcely heard. He had turned to the last pages of Alan's notes, to the name that had flicked by in the moment before Pippa handed him Jo's scrawled note. The heading read *Thomas Garland,* with the note "Not much known outside of scraps from parish registers, Revels accounts, legal documents, &c., &c. Boiled down it amounts to:

Born 1576 (??) in Kilburn (?).
Mentioned in the list of Choristers of St. Paul's when their
        theatre reopened in 1587. Would have been 11. In
        1590 pamphlet attacking the Children of Paul's was
        probably the *Tom Long-stamps, the Kylburn*

swadder's son who struts it calflike in his spangles
and setts the silly ninihammers all a-sigh.

In the '90s when the choristers' theatres were closed down must have been acting somewhere & doing fairly well, for in

1600—appears as one of the sharers when Henry Evans leased the fencing theatre at Blackfriars for the Children of the Chapel Royal.

1601—appeared for the first time with the Lord Chamberlain's Men—in Shakespeare's *Troilus and Cressida*.

1602—married Katherine, daughter of Henry Purfet, a clockmaker in Kingston-on-Thames.

1603—when the Lord Chamberlain's Men were reorganised as the King's Men, Garland paid Burbage £80 to come in as sharer when the number of shares was increased—but the King wanted his own man Laurence Fletcher in. G. may have been promised the next vacancy, as there seems to be no record of the £80 being returned.

In fact, no further record of him at all. Irons suggests he may have been the player in Dekker's tragic tale of the young man found dead of the plague at the Blue Pump. John Taylor the Water Poet included the Blue Pump in his 1630 list of taverns, and Rendle's *Old Southwark* says it was once called "Poor Tom's Last Refuge" (!!)

Roger turned the page slowly. And there it was.

T.G. could be related (brother?) to the Jack Garland who in 1600 is one of the boy players in Evans' Chapel Royal company at Blackfriars.

J.G. seems to have been involved in scandal of the 8 children kidnapped to be players. Not clear how. Turns up as apprentice (his brother's?) with the King's Men in 1602, probably 13–14 then.

108

Nothing in theatre histories to connect T.G. with Isleworth,
but other members of Shakesp's company did move
out that way—to Mortlake (Phillips), Brentford
(Lowin), & Cundall at some point to Fulham.

"Roger? What's the matter?" Pippa asked. She pushed
Sammy firmly away and came round the table. "What
is it?"

"Old Alan's found us another ghost, Pips." Roger tried
to sound jaunty but it came out in a shaky whisper. "Me."

Pippa refused to budge from Roger's side for the rest
of the evening, and when it came time to go upstairs he
was secretly grateful. Jemima had been given his new
bed in the little downstairs room; Alan when he came
would have a camp bed downstairs; and Pippa's room was
already crowded with its bed and animals or Roger would
have smothered his pride and set his camp bed up there.
He was left with the master bedroom willy-nilly and was
absurdly, ashamedly thankful when Pippa appeared in the
doorway in her pyjamas with the canvas roll and metal
legs of her own camp bed in her arms. She calmly set
about putting it together in the dressing-room alcove and
shook her head firmly when Roger objected that she was
leaving an excellent and un-slept-in bed for that canvas
sling. "It's too scary to be all by myself," she said stub-
bornly. She was actually asleep not five minutes after
wriggling down into the sleeping bag.

It was not so easy for Roger. He took a long, warm
soak in the bath, pulling the plug and towelling dry only
when Jo's sharp rap on the door brought his father's illness and his own helplessness in the face of it flooding
back. He half dressed again, and in the bedroom unrolled

his sleeping bag on the floor and sat with his back against the fireplace wall—sat, and picked over the pieces of his frightening puzzle one by one.

Perhaps there was no ghost at all. Not, at least, in the way Pippa meant, in the familiar sense of an unquiet spirit haunting an unhappy place. For how could the house *itself* have a ghost? The house he had seen had once been real—there was the old staircase to prove that— but it was a thing, and things did not have ghosts. Tony— and he—had not gone sleepwalking through the ghost of St. John's Wood when it was still a wood, but in the place itself. By some strange shift past and present there had run together, overlapped even, so that Tony had walked in both at once. "How" hardly mattered. Sleepwalking, waking, or dreaming, it was the same. Tony had gone all the way, past Tyburn to the City, and only half come back. He had neither heard Tom Garland's grief nor seen his house as it once had been, yet he had been drawn into the shadow where the two times touched. And still was there, fast slipping out of reach. This flu—if it were flu—left him no defences. *And me? I'm all defences,* Roger thought bitterly.

Oh, yes. He, as much as his father, had been claimed by the old tale that had left so much pain in Castle Cox, but he was too much on guard against surprise and change and loss, too intent on sidestepping the shadows that fell across his path, backing away from what he feared like a wary, wild animal, to be caught. Listening in the hallway at Hamilton Terrace that morning he had heard his father say just that: like a wild animal. And Tony? Tony was on guard against nothing, no one. Curious, generous, careless—loving—and short-tempered, he met everything head on. Roger envied that blind innocence and yet ... and yet because of it his father had fallen headlong into the old tale.

Pippa made a comfortable little noise in her sleep and, turning, nestled down like a curled-up kitten. Watching from what felt like a great distance, Roger felt an unaccustomed surge of feeling, unreasoned and overwhelming. "I love you, Pips," he whispered. "I really do. Jo too."

But Jack had hated Katherine, Tom's "Kitten." Hated and meant to be rid of her. Meant to be at the centre of Tom's world again no matter what the cost. And so he did a dreadful thing.

And Roger, caught off guard at last, sat in a shaft of moonlight and remembered.

*I haue shot my arrowe
ore the house
And hurt my brother*

ACK GARLAND CUT A NEAT SLICE from the loaf he and little Bob Somercote were sharing and topped it with a slice of cheese. Bob still worked on the chicken-back, as if the bird would yield up another morsel or two to perseverance. Bob was twelve, but slow to learn his graces. Jack watched his busy, greasy progress for a moment with distaste but then was far away once more, rapt in a fantasy that made his dark eyes gleam and his breath draw tight and shallow.

Katherine dead. Dead of the plague and already buried. It was possible. He had not thought there would be so much sickness outside the City and Southwark, where last week near two thousand had died. Yet here at the Lion the tables and benches were still half-empty at the tag-end of suppertime and the air was full of uneasy rumours: too many Cits come west trailing infection after them, more houses fresh-marked for quarantine each day, and Isleworth worse than Brentford and Twickenham together. Yes, it was possible. Katherine tumbled into a wide, shallow grave, her long blonde hair cut off and sold to stuff a mattress . . .

"Jack, *leave off!*" Bob's whisper was a hiss. "Or we must pay for the table too. The host has the look of a thunder-cloud about to burst."

Coming to himself, Jack saw that in his daydream he had stuck his knife deep into the oaken trestle and pried up a heavy splinter. He met the landlord's narrowed gaze across the room with a flushed, blank stare, pried a little harder, and then let the splinter snap loudly home. He wiped his knife carefully and sheathed it, turning back to his bread and cheese and ale. As he turned, his eye was caught by a wineglass raised in salute from a bench by the open window.

"Who are those?" Bob asked. "I've seen 'em at the play-house, ha'n't I?"

Jack shrugged and took a long, thirsty swallow from his tankard. "The fair bearded one in green silk is Harry Cliffe, a law student at the Temple or one of the Inns of Court. The others too, I think. A time or three they bought seats on the stage and played at being rude and lordly. They're naught but pint-pots."

"He looks to catch your eye. What's the harm?" Bob asked in an eager undertone. "If you'll at least be civil, I'll play sweet-ten-and-bashful. We'll diddle 'em into paying for our supper."

Jack gave him a cold stare. "Wipe your chin, you greasy little apple-squire. If ever my coin won't stretch to my supper, I've credit here. They know Tom." He made a sign to the drawer, who was busying himself collecting empty ale-pots, and that unfortunate went scurrying in search of the host.

"I'd best go," Jack said. "The furnishings and clothes for the tour'll be loaded by now and will be coming up from the Globe before long with the mid-tide. I mean to be home before Tom, and you'd be wise to go be sweet-and-bashful with Mistress Lowin before old John comes home. And remember, you pudding-brain: we didn't go scavengin' in empty houses. We walked to Putney, took the ferry, ate too much, and then slept until dusk in the Bishop's orchard. Agreed?"

The landlord, fetched by the drawer, appeared to give the boys their reckoning, and Jack carefully counted the three shillings from his purse. When the man was out of earshot once again, he added, "And you mind your step with Cliffe, or you'll have your ears trimmed. He's an Essex man, but if he's here, he's lodged with the Earl of Northumberland at Syon House. His mother, 'tis said, was connected with the Percies, so he's some sort of kin."

"Oh," Bob said, subsiding. "A large pint-pot."

Jack laughed as he rose and shouldered his leather travelling box. "Just so. I'll see you next week at Mortlake when it's time to set off for Oxford. Mind your ears!"

Jack did not hurry. He was tired and, allowing for the tide, there was no need. He should reach New House an hour or so before Tom came. It was a lucky chance that early that morning he had overheard Mr. Lowin's remark to Mr. Phillips that "young Garland ought to come to me till Monday next, give his brother some time with that pretty wife. I'll mention it to Tom." So he most probably had, but not in time. For soon after—as soon as it was clear that the stage furnishings and costumes for the tour would not be packed for loading by ten, in time for the strong mid-tide flow—Jack and his box had taken off with Bob and left the work to the others. Tom would never dislodge him once he was comfortably settled in, and Katherine was too soft-hearted to be anything but kind and welcoming.

Perhaps she was, but there was no comfort in that. It was for her that Tom was pouring every penny that he made into the newly-finished house at Isleworth. His share in the Blackfriars theatre had been a profitable investment, and now that he'd been promised the next vacancy among the sharers of the Globe he spoke more and more often of wanting children, and of the pleasant country-village life to be had on the edge of a great estate—as if he would happily give up their lodgings in Bankside and spend the whole of the year out here at the edge of the world! It was hard enough in plague-time, when all who could went into the country. How could he think of leaving the noise, the surge of life, the smells for good? For this chirruping of crickets and lowing of cows? How could he?

Only, of course, because his Kitten liked it. In Southwark respectable grocers and housewives and school-masters had to rub elbows with rogues and doxies and rufflers. In Southwark, two or three poor souls from the White Lion or the Bench Prisons were hung each day from the street-gallows, offal was thrown in the stinking ditches, and church-going landlords made tidy profits from the Bankside bawdy-houses. Pretty little Kate from quiet Kingston hated it.

Well, he hated quiet Kate and the soft, aching, doting way Tom looked at her and had no time for any other if she were there. He'd scarce said three words in a row to Jack these weeks past beyond those to do with work—a fencing lesson given, or a song or speech for Jack to learn—and it was all for mooning over Katherine, sent safe away from the plaguey town to New House. At least Katherine would not have him for long: a scant week only, thank heaven. Plague may have closed the playhouses, but players must eat, so on Tuesday next they were to leave from Augustine Phillips' at Mortlake on the first leg of a tour that would take *Hamlet, The Merry Devil of Edmonton, The London Prodigal,* and three other plays to Oxford, Bath, Shrewsbury, Coventry, Cambridge, Ipswich, and towns between.

The Syon meadow road's long curve towards the river Thames brought Jack before long to the New House lane along the old Wardenhold parsonage wall, and he was halfway down its length before the silence caught his ear. There was no racket of alarm from Fawn and Buff, the dogs who guarded the lane and house so jealously that after a long absence even Tom was suspect. Dogs, Jack knew, were being killed as plague-bearers in the City and Westminster, but—here? He broke into a run.

But no, there was no cross daubed on the door, no despairing *Lord, Haue Mercie uppon Vs* printed on a quarantine placard. Jack felt a faint guilty twinge of relief. Perhaps he did not truly wish Katherine dead— only to be shed of her. Recovering himself, he knocked at the nail-studded door in loud impatience.

There was no answer. If there was no plague sign, neither was there light in any window or a maidservant to come running at his knock. Something *was* wrong, and it took a maddening time in the fading light to find the iron key in his box, and then to fit it in the lock. Once in, he groped along the shadowy oak chest beside the door for the candlestick kept there and, finding it, struck a light.

The wide, wainscoted hall was oddly bare. The table-carpets, pewter and plate, the little piles of books, and pretty plants in pots—all the movables—were gone, leaving only the heavy furniture and the rush mats on the floor.

"Katherine? Molly? Molly, you slut, where are you?"

The house was deserted, the kitchen and larder stripped, the linenfold shutters in the ground floor windows fastened. His own room upstairs looked untouched, but there was a note propped against his pillow. *My dere brother*, it read, *I haue taken your siluer mirour & siluer backt combe wth mee to Kyngston for safe kepyng & I shal hope itt will not be longe tyll I see you theyr wth oure dere Tom. Yo^r lovyng sister Katherine.*

To Kingston? Home to her family? Why? And with his silver comb and mirror! As to that, she was probably right, though not having them to hand was irksome. An empty house drew thieves. Jack grinned at the thought of the houses he and Bob had rummaged through in Lambeth, and the silver spoons rolled up in his spare hose in the leather box. But why should she flee this comfort for a house crowded with brothers and sisters, servants, and her father's 'prentices?

There was another note, bulkier and sealed, propped

117

against one of the embroidered pillowcases on Tom's and her own bed beside a nosegay of wilted, drying flowers. Taking up the letter, Jack set the candlestick on the chest at the bed's foot, drew his knife and after heating the thin blade, ran it neatly under the letter's seal. Unfolded, it proved to be four pages in Katherine's painstakingly neat hand, and he skimmed through them quickly.

My onely dere swete harte. I am sore distrest that you sh^d come hoame & finde mee gone for all these weekes I haue longyd onely to be wth you. I haue no othyr comforte but to see you &knowe yor loue swete harte & I pray All mighty god th^t yor rehersalls haue gon well & you are safely come hoame to read thys. You must knowe th^t if I do not stay for yor comming itt is becos in Istleworth the syknes grows so gret th^t I am feared to stay. XXX or XL are dead th^t I knowe of & more who are kept secret so theyr howses be not shut upp & theyr people stopped from comming & goeing. & the syknes goes euerywhere euene to the mayds att Mr Plums for hys moat wyl nott kepe Deth oute. The curate & Mr Moris & som othyrs sey itt is the paper mille th^t is the cause of the gret syknes here for gret loades of raggs & cloathing come upp eche tide from the Cittie to be made into paper & itt is sayd they are cloathes & linnens from infected howses & poore ded folk. Mr Moris sayes itt is agaynst the Cittie law but here nott.

My derest I pratle on becos I feare you haue not had my letters sence I haue had none from you these weekes. I feare you are stille angrey wth mee for walkyng wth that man in Sion fielde but what could I do when hee would followe mee so boldely & nott let goe my hand? I was soe happy when you came & rescued mee for hee would not beleeve I was maryed & then to haue you thynke it my fault was hard to beare. I am shamed to tell you now th^t in my hurtt I did not giue you the gret good newes th^t come October we are to haue a chyld, god

willyng. It is soe wonderfull newes th I am shamed now to*
haue kept itt from you & my mother wrote to chide mee for itt.
Now shee & my father hearying how evill the syknes is in
thys place haue sent theyr seruant wth the waggon to Kew &
Istleworth ferry to bryng mee hoame to theym in Kyngston
wher itt is not soe bad. I do not wish to goe but my father seys
itt is my dutie to you to kepe safe my selfe & childe. Do not I
pray you tary at New Howse. I looke for you to come quick
as you may.

Jack turned to the fourth sheet where Katherine ended
in a hasty scrawl:

Ile say farwell then Tom sence the man is waityng for mee
thoughe thys letter is too shorte for all th I woulde saye. I*
ende prayenge allmighty god blesse you for his mercies sacke
& prayenge yor forgifnes for my sad deceipt.
                    Yo^r woefulle Kitten

Jack stared blindly at the pages trembling in his hand.
He shivered uncontrollably, his eyes blurring with angry
tears. A brat. The bitch was going to have a brat and next
year there would be another and where would he be then?
Alone in lodgings on Bankside with his room at New
House readied for even more of the mewing, smelly
things. The beautiful room had been his for only the two
short months since the house was finished, and though
it might not be in London Town, it was *his*. And Tom.
Dear rackety Tom would grow thick-waisted and tame,
become a vestryman at All Saints' and dote so on his
growing family that he would scarce spare a thought for
brother Jack who once had been the apple of his eye.

Unless...*unless*...Jack wiped his eyes and looked
again at the fourth sheet. Almost—almost it had by itself

119

the look of a hasty note. *A farewell note*. If it were read in haste. . . .

It was the mention of that nasty scene in Syon Field that gave him the idea. Katherine had gone to Syon Garden to watch Tom and William Percy rehearse the lords and ladies in their speeches and dances for *The Fairy Pastorall*, the masque Percy had written for entertainment at the great banquet the Earl was to give for the King on the eighth of June. Young Harry Cliffe had seen her there and followed when she slipped out to walk home through the pretty tree-shaded pasture, but jealous, sharp-eyed Tom had read Cliffe's hungry look and was not far behind. It had come almost to blows, with Cliffe sneering that no low-born, ranting player could hope to keep such a pretty piece to himself, and Tom tearing strips off his hide with words as keen as knives. Cliffe would have liked to run him through for that, unarmed or no, but may have been unsure of Tom's standing with the King's Men, for he held his anger in check. The Globe playhouse sharers by their charter literally were "King's Men"—Gentlemen of the Bedchamber to King James and privileged as such, low-born or no.

But if Cliffe backed off, he had not forgotten Katherine. Twice on Bankside he had sought Jack out to offer him a fat and tempting purse of gold for putting him in the way of speaking with her away from New House and the maid and manservant. That he meant to abduct her Jack was sure, but he dared not help, for Kitten's tale of his part in such a plot would surely come in time to Tom. But this now . . . this might be safe. If Cliffe would play his part in exchange for word of where Katherine was and how he might come at her. . . .

There was not much time. An hour, perhaps, if that. Swiftly Jack re-heated his knife blade to seal up the fourth sheet of the letter by itself, and when it was done he replaced the folded paper against the pillow. Tom in his haste would never notice the smeared edge of the sealing wax. What next? A quick look in Katherine's fripperie told him she had left a dress or two behind. It would not matter in the dark that they were her shabbiest. Jack took up the candle and hurried out and down the stairs, pausing briefly on the landing. There was no time to burn the three pages he still held, so he put down the candlestick and tugged upward at the great round knob of the newel post. He had found the shallow hiding-place when it came loose by accident one day, and since then a little wedge of paper had kept it tight and secret. There was just room for the much-folded papers on top of his small hoard of money.

In the next minute he was out the door and hurrying back to the Lion, this time not the long way round by the road, but over the gate into Syon Field and racing north through the summer-dry grass.

The coming back was faster yet. Cliffe took Jack up behind him on the bay gelding and passed Syon gate-house at a canter, putting the horse at the field gate as if it were no higher than a joint-stool. In mid-field he pulled up among the trees. "I'll ride to meet you when I see y'at the far side," he said shortly. Jack was almost glad the dusk beneath the trees obscured the young man's exultant grin.

Back in his own room at New House Jack stripped to his small-clothes, bundling the doublet and trunk-hose into a worn old cloak-bag of Katherine's. The muslin dress was an uncomfortably tight fit across his shoulders—his costume for *The London Prodigal* would have been perfect but this would have to serve, fastened at the bodice-front or no. A handkerchief pinned there would hide the gap. From his own box he drew the two wig bags and looked in each to find the blonde one. A few loosened pins, a deft twist or two, and when he slipped it on it transformed him not into a lady of the Danish Court, but a passable sort of Katherine. He had two pairs of ladies' shoes as well, but decided to keep to his own in case he had to run for it. The shoes, the rest of his own clothing, and his makeup box he crammed into the cloak-bag. The leather box he pushed out of sight beneath his bed.

Tom Garland, when the waterman put him ashore at the ferry landing, came past the church and up the road in long, impatient strides, his box upon his back and a bulky parcel wrapped with coarse muslin and twine under his arm. He had come no further than the first gate into Syon Field and the Wardenhold parsonage opposite when twenty yards ahead he saw a figure in a pale dress move into the moonlight from New House lane, waver uncertainly, and then hurry away with a distinctive, familiar skimming gait, half walk and half run.

Kitten! Out at night? And alone? He could have felt no more than bewildered at first, but he had dropped his burdens in the lane and followed. What he must have felt at seeing her throw a cloak-bag over the next Syon Field gate and go nimbly after it, full skirt, farthingale and all, or at recognizing the horseman who cantered up to meet her, Jack could not imagine. Anger surely, then betrayal. Pain. And then disgust. To be cruelly sure, Cliffe laughed and bent to kiss "Kitten's" hands.

"Dearest Kitty-Kate," Cliffe said in a laughing, carrying voice. "The boatmen wait at Syon Wharf. We must be away before your foolish husband comes. My baggage waits us at the Temple. Here, let me hand you up."

And then the horse was drumming away, leaving poor Tom Garland rooted by the gate, caught fast in the long nightmare.

That if againe this apparifion come

SO LONG AGO. IT HAD HAPPENED SO long ago. But in this room in this house it seemed scarcely a day ago, an hour ago.

"Are you all right?" A whisper.

Roger came out of his reverie to find Pippa, sitting up in her sleeping bag, watching him doubtfully. "I was just remembering," he said slowly.

And he told her.

"I don't know whether I *can* explain it," Roger said unhappily when he had finished. Pippa lay curled on her side watching him, accepting the tale of Jack and Tom matter-of-factly, without wonder, without questions. "I don't know whether it's explainable."

But he wanted very much to understand, and so he tried. "Look: thinking about the past we usually think about certain people in this story or that out of times past, not about *all* the things that were going on in that minute. Well, maybe a patch of time can be something like a theatre. The audience is in the present, coming and going, eating and drinking and talking, and looking at the past up there on the stage. But suppose there were seats up on the stage too, the way there were in Tom's time. And that's this house. Anyway, while you sit there you feel inside the play on one side, and still part of the audience on the other, and you know that if you weren't afraid to break the rules you could leave your chair and be a player in the past yourself..." He paused, unsure. "No, maybe that's not it at all. But it's the way it *feels*."

"That's awfully complicated," Pippa said doubtfully. "Maybe it's *how*, but it doesn't tell why. If poor Tom's heart was that broken maybe he just goes on looking for her and forever and over dying in the plague—didn't Alan's notebook say he might've? And he's using Tony to help look."

But Roger shied away from anything so alarmingly direct as a ghost—and at that a ghost who desperately and endlessly sought a truth that *he* knew. "I suppose it could come to the same thing," he said uncomfortably. He fell into an unhappy silence.

Into that silence came the sound of a car's motor and, after a moment, the front door closing and the murmur of voices below. The door across the way closed quietly and Jo's footsteps whispered towards the hall stairs.

"Alan's back," Roger said. He felt in the dark shadow on the floor beside him for his sandals. "You stay here. I'll see what Jo says about how Pa's feeling."

He meant to join Jo and Jemima and Alan in the front room, but when he came to the bottom of the stairs he heard Jo's quiet voice saying, "No, I've not looked at it. I've been too occupied with Tony. But Jemima did tell me a little. You don't actually think Thomas Garland's *haunting* this house, do you? It sounds quite absurd."

Roger stopped and stood quite still.

"Of course it is," Alan agreed. "But it did have me going for a while. That colloquial Elizabethan accent, the way Tony changed, the confusion between past and present— I had some pretty crazy ideas going. But on the way up to town it hit me: here's a chap under a tremendous strain who walks into a house straight out of his childhood fantasies. Who's to say that didn't stir up some long-forgotten tale of poor Tom's ghost? If Coxes lived here as long as Tony seems to think, they might have picked up any old stories that were passed down along with the house. An actor who played on the same stage with Shakespeare and may have died in a plague epidemic *would* be remembered in a village the size this must have been, and Tony's gran or his aunt could have told him the last few tatters of the tale when he was too young to think it interesting."

"It's just possible," Jemima said with cautious interest. "On one of the maps I copied bits from this morning there *was* something. Just a minute..." Her footsteps hurried into the dining room and came tapping back. "Here it is. This one was dated 1627. This house is marked 'New House'—though it's shown as L-shaped—

but there's no owner's name given as there are on these others. There is a 'Coxes' though. Up here beyond where the road used to turn north towards Brentford before it was straightened and cut up through the Town Field to the London Road."

"Well there you are, then," Alan said happily. That's it. Nursery tales have an uncanny way of surviving for centuries."

"I'm not sure it's one Tony would have forgotten if ever he did hear it," Jo said mildly. "It's true we haven't heard anything out of the way these past two nights while he was up in town.... But I can't worry about all this now. Tony's asleep at last, but his breathing sounds dreadful and his pulse seems slow. He said not, but I wonder whether we oughtn't look up a doctor to root out of bed. I don't like to ask you to go out again, Alan, but since we're so close to West Middlesex Hospital, I thought you might zip around and ask whether they have a list of local doctors who are on call."

"Dear Jo," Alan protested. "Why didn't you say so straightaway? I thought you were looking rather haunted, but I'm a little slow on the uptake at this hour." There was the sound of the canvas chair scraping back as he pushed up out of it. "If I see a stray doctor passing the reception desk, I shall abduct him on the spot. What do I say if I'm asked Tony's temperature?"

"One hundred and one. That was fifteen or twenty minutes ago."

"Right." Alan emerged into the hallway and caught sight of Roger standing rooted in the shadows there. "Good grief, you startled me, Rog." His voice dropped as he opened the front door, "I say, be a good lad and don't let Jo see you looking so tragic. I'm off to fetch a doctor. Back in a trice."

Roger could not face Jo. His feelings were in too much of a turmoil. He fled upstairs instead, to Pippa and the ghost-filled room. Oh, yesterday he would have embraced Alan's theory wholeheartedly. But even if he had not learned the truth since then, he would have known that Jo was right: if his father had been told at the age of *three* that Castle Cox had once belonged to one of Shakespeare's actors, he would quite probably have remembered every word of it.

There was a great deal of coming and going in the upstairs hall in the hour that followed, and nothing Roger and Pippa could do but leave the door ajar and keep out from underfoot. Roger found himself nodding where he sat, and gathered up his sleeping bag to spread it on the second camp bed. He could not sleep, but fell into a half-doze where the doctor's murmured, "rather nasty inflammation of the throat . . ." and ". . . see whether this doesn't make him more comfortable," were mixed with a strange and distant female voice saying, "You've a touch of it yourself, my lad, by the look of you," and Jo's muffled, "I think the hall is wide enough, but they'll just have to bring it on up to be sure." It was two in the morning when he was roused by Jemima's hand on his shoulder.

"Don't be alarmed, love. The ambulance is here to take your dad to the hospital, and Jo thought you'd want to know. Close the door behind you. No need to wake Pippa."

The ambulance trolley stood in the hall and the two attendants were helping Tony onto it. The doctor left

Jo's side to stand beside Tony as one man covered him with a light blanket and fastened the straps. "Have they made you comfortable enough, Mr. Nicholas?"

"Hurts all over," Tony murmured indistinctly. "Dam' silly nuisance."

"Pa?" Roger moved quickly as the trolley was rolled to the head of the stairs, and touched his father's arm. "Don't worry," he said softly. " 'Go on, I'll follow thee.' "

No one else seemed to hear, but Tony's eyes fastened on him in an intent, unfocussed way. "Jack?" he whispered. "No, not Jack . . ."

"What did he say?" asked the doctor as the ambulance attendants took up the weight of the trolley and started down the stairs. "Roger, is it? Roger, did you catch what your father said?"

"Nothing really. I don't know. Jo?" He turned. "Do— do you want me to come with you in the ambulance?"

Jo rubbed her eyes wearily. "Only if you'd like. Alan's going to follow to bring me back once Tony's more comfortable, but Jemima will be here in case Pippa wakes. Do you want to come?" She waited on the top step.

"Not if you don't need me." Roger looked back toward the bedroom door. "I've something else to do."

Only later, in the ambulance, did Jo think what an odd answer it was for two in the morning.

The house slid into sleep at last, Pippa, Jemmy, even Roger for a while, though he struggled to keep awake. For it was here that Tom would come. Must come. Tony slept where he was safe from walking, so it was here that Tom must come. Must.

But when he came, pale with hurt and anger, throwing

129

wide the lost door from the old stair passage and hurling his muslin-wrapped parcel onto the chest at the bed's foot, both Roger and Pippa were lost in sleep. His candle cast its glimmer across their dreams, but neither woke to see him snatch the letter, break the seal, and scan those few lines that tumbled all his hopes that the woman he had seen had not been Katherine.

The low, moaning grief that had wakened him on the first night echoed at last in Roger's dream, but waking this time was an even deeper struggle than that first. He swam upward from a great, dark depth, and when his eyes at last dragged open it was at the sound of the front door's heavy slam. What he saw was the great bed with its embroidered linen hangings, and the crumpled letter lying on the coverlet. The parcel's wrappings were strewn across the floor, and on the chest a peach-flower-and-corn-coloured gown of tissue silk and light brocade hung grotesquely to the floor, its pinked sleeves with silver bone lace ripped from the bodice, and the wide frounced skirt torn down through its silken roses to the hem.

Roger sat up in alarm, feeling half shadow himself on the shadowy camp bed, and swung his feet to the dark, polished floor. Tom . . . Tom had come and gone. How was he to tell him, to warn him, now? How follow? Roger rose and crossed to the bed, meaning to smooth out the paper and take it with him, but his fingers only stirred it slightly, as if he were no more than a faint disturbance in that older place. Touch, feeling—they were there, but he felt as queerly insubstantial as a child in the fever of some illness, powerless and muffled up in silence.

Roger looked around him wildly. He had not understood. He had not thought it through. For, what was he here, in this older place, but a ghost? A ghost out of the future, but a ghost no less. How was he to unravel the web that Jack had spun if he could not even pick up a little piece of paper? How could he hope to unwedge the newel post and retrieve the other sheets? And without them, how much of the tale would Tom believe? Roger hurried into the moonlit passage and plunged downward, the broad rail smooth under his hand, to the newel post on the landing, a dark, polished globe as smooth and vivid to the touch as silk. But to grasp it, to get some purchase on it, was like trying to pick up a bead of mercury between one's fingers—impossible.

In his desperation he did not hear the heavy front door open again and close, nor the sharp little scratch of noise that followed it. He was caught like a rabbit dazzled by torchlight when a candle flared alight, standing frozen with his arms around the newel knob. Jack stood below, on the rush mat by the door, shading the guttering candle with his hand. He had rid himself of the dress, and in his doublet of claret-coloured silk, and mouse-grey sleeves and hose, with his thin, arrogant face and dark tousled curls, looked like a painted figure from an Elizabethan miniature eerily come to life.

"Ho! Who's to home?" he called, with a wry quirk of an eyebrow. "Tom? Sister Katherine?" When no answer came from Tom, he stepped nervously across the gleaming floor toward the stairs. "Tom? Who's here? 'Tis you, isn't it?"

Roger did not move for fear of frightening him away. *If you're not afraid to break the rules ... you can cross that line and be a player in the past yourself.* Perhaps he had known all along what it must come to. Only Jack could mend what Jack had broken. Only Jack could stitch up this ragged rent in the curtain between past and present. Only Jack.

At the foot of the stairs Jack slowed suddenly and held the candle high. "Who's there? I—" His glimmer of fear turned to fury. "Who are you? *Get away from that post* whoever you are! 'Tis *my* gold in there, all I've saved, and you'll not dip your fambles in't." Shifting the candlestick to his left hand he took the stairs two at a time, drawing his knife as he came.

But on the landing he saw at last that the shadow by the newel post was more a shadow than a man.

"Who.... What is't you want?" he faltered. "Who are you?" As Roger let go the post-knob to move towards him, he stumbled backwards into the corner of the landing, stammering, "No, n-no."

Roger reached out in alarm toward the wavering candlestick.

"Please, no." The words were scarce a whisper.

Pippa watching numbly from above, saw the two figures blur and merge until they moved as one, carefully placing the candlestick out of the way in a corner of the landing. The shape was Roger and not-Roger, both flesh and blood and shadow. It stepped to the newel post to grasp it as Roger had done, worked loose the great knob, and pulled it free. From the deep socket it drew some folded papers, stuffed them inside the claret-coloured doublet, took up the candlestick once more, and hurried down the stairs.

Goe on, Ile followe thee

H E HAD THOUGHT IT WOULD FEEL strange, but it did not. The candle was snuffed, the door locked, and Roger was over the threshold into New House lane, bent for the river and the ferryman's house. Surprisingly, more than anything it felt like coming home to a place one had known years before —oddly vivid and strange in its familiarity. He knew that he must find a boat. Tom would try first for Syon Wharf, and then for Temple Stairs in town. And if there were no watermen putting up for the night at the ferryman's cottage, no boat to be had? He could swim as far as Syon Wharf or look for a horse to hire to town. Or walk.

Money. How much was the hire of a boat? Roger felt at his waist and found the purse hanging there. Not much. A dozen or so smallish coins. Why had he not thought that he would need money when his hand touched the coins inside the newel post? It was too late now. Pray God he had enough.

Coming round the curve of road past the church, Roger saw a yellow glow wink out in a window of the timbered cottage at the water's edge where the flat-bottomed ferry was moored and broke into a run. In the dooryard he was brought up short, cracking his shin on one of the benches where Mrs. Fairman served wine and ale and bread and cheese to travellers. *"Mrs. Fairman"? Where had that come from?* The noise and his muffled exclamation roused a terrier who came scrambling out from among the wharf pilings with a piercing, angry yap as alarming as any bulldog's growl.

"Who's there? 'Tis too late t' cross tonight." The light sprang up again, and a wicket in the cottage door opened a crack. "Who's there, I say? Ah, 'tis you, Master Garland. What is't you're after?"

"Has my brother come this way, Mr. Fairman?" Will Fairman. The man's name came as easily as his face was familiar.

"Aye right, he did. And took away John Tomasin, who was enjoyin' a pipe and a bottle and a good tale or two away from his old woman—who's a terror, I hear, and fearful company now she's paid by the magistrates to go viewin' corpses so's the plaguey ones aren't passed off as clean to 'scape the quarantine. Right cruel it was to take 'im back to Lunnon so suddenlike. Indeed—"

Roger cut in firmly. "Did he *say* 'to London,' Mr. Fair-

134

man? And was it John Tomasin who brought him up from Bankside?"

"It was. But as for Lunnon I couldn't swear. Thinkin' on it now you ask, may be he said no more'n 'down river.' In a hurry, he was, for he—"

"Mr. Fairman, I'm in a hurry too. Are any of Tomasin's fellows laid up here for the night?"

"No lad, there's not." Mr. Fairman scratched his beard consideringly. "But if you've a borde or three in that bung of yours, you're welcome to that sweet little skiff tied upstream from the ferry."

It was as sour-looking a little pram dinghy as Roger had ever seen, but it had oars, and not above a half-inch of water slopping in the bottom. Roger came back to Mr. Fairman and the candlelight to finger through his purse. Three shillings was steep—absurdly so if he found Tom at Syon—but since there was no knowing when or whether the boat would come to Isleworth again, he gave the man a gold crown and left him staring in disbelief.

The moon was rising still, and when Roger pushed out from the shadows of the ferry and the tree-clad ait, he found himself riding the silvered river in a world of cricket song and night-birds and the quiet lap-slap of barely moving water touching boat and bank. As soon as he was clear of the ferry he sculled half round with an oar over the stern, then fixed the oars in the rowlocks and bent his back to pull hard downstream.

The work felt good and he was good at it —it was far too long since he had been on the river! He rowed a true, fast course between mid-channel and Syon water meadows where the silvery reeds were full of sleeping swans and

135

drank it in with wonder. Too long? He gave a grunt of laughter as he pulled. In a manner of speaking, it was the very first time he had been on the Thames. Those other times were centuries yet to come.

As the little boat drew abreast of Syon Wharf and landing stairs, Roger saw that they were chained off and deserted. Up across the pasture the great turreted three-storied house shone pale above its garden walls, one window lit where scant weeks ago every one had blazed with candles. So. No watchman even, who might have been bribed to delay Tom with hemming and hawing over which gentleman and lady had taken a wherry for where. Roger bent his back to the oars again, moving into the deep channel and rowing steadily but more slowly, for Mortlake was a good long pull downstream. It was not likely that Tom in his haste would stop there, but it was possible, and there was Katherine to think of, too. She must be warned. One of Tom's friends must take word to Kingston.

He was rowing now in slack water, the pause between the flow and ebb tides. The tide would soon be turning and the going easier. As Roger bent and pulled, bent and pulled, he began to wonder. Mr. Fairman...Syon all ablaze with candles...he even knew that John Tomasin the waterman had deep pock-marks on his cheeks, wore an earring, and had his boat upholstered in green and gold. But if he knew what Jack knew, why then did so much—the moon on the beautiful river, the curving sweep of tree-clad banks, the sleeping swans—seem so new, so never-seen?

Beyond the tiny village of Strand-on-the-Green, Mortlake slept among the trees on the opposite bank. Rather,

136

most of it slept. Pulling ashore beyond the town wharf, Roger moored the little boat to a tree on the bank and made his way toward the inn and the sound of music. Through the open front door he saw Bob Armin, arms flung wide, leading the refrain to "Friar Foxtail." Jack Wilson's dark head was bent over his guitar, and others sat on the benches circled round them, singing and laughing: Bob Goffe, Ned, Sam Gilburne and Sam Crosse. Roger hesitated—a more cheerfully gossippy lot would be hard to come by. If they learned how Tom had been diddled, Tom would never hear the end of it.

"With the players, are ye?" The voice came from a bench under a dooryard tree, where the small red glow from a pipe brightened as the speaker took a puff. "Sorry, lad, I didn't mean to startle ye. I'm landlord here, and when I've finished my pipe I'll be packin' 'em off to their lodgings, for I'll not have 'em sleeping till noon on my benches. Is't one o' them ye're after?"

"No. Tom Garland. Do you know him?"

"Aye, to see him. But he's not been here. You'll do best to ask at Mr. Phillips' in the morning."

"Yes," Roger said uncertainly, turning away. "Thank you."

"Aye, good night to ye, lad."

At Augustine Phillips' the front of the house was dark, but from the lane down along the side garden, Roger caught a glimpse of light at a window. A servant seeing to the locks and shutters, most likely. But still, a servant would know if Tom had been there. Boldly, Roger vaulted the low hedge and made his way among the box trees and borders to the window where the light still glowed.

"They're all abed, young Garland."

Roger whirled in alarm to see the shadow of a man in the deeper shade of a medlar tree. "Angels and ministers of grace defend us!" he quavered. "Who's there?"

The man moved into the moonlight, his voice coolly amused, but not friendly. "An apt greeting, Jack. But I did not mean to be rehearsing the ghost of Hamlet's father. I may 'revisit thus the glimpses of the moon' but I trust I do not 'make night hideous.'"

"No, sir. You startled me, but I w-was not skulking," Roger stammered. "I didn't wish to rouse the house. I hoped to catch a servant, sir, or one of the 'prentices."

"To ask after Tom? He's been and gone not half an hour past. He stormed in like a madman, borrowed three pounds of me, wrote a line or two to be taken tomorrow to his father-in-law in Kingston, and was gone."

Roger's heart sank. "Did he say what he meant to do?"

"No, nor what had 'mazed him so." Dark, keen eyes skewered Roger. "If your fine hand is in it, Jack, and it comes to ill, we'll see you never tread another stage. We took you on for Tom's sake. We would as happily be rid of you for it."

Roger scarcely heard. If Tom had written to Kingston in his first shock and anger, Mr. Purfet, Katherine's father would never make head nor tail of it. And Katherine would be in danger. What use was anything if she were lost?

"Have you pen and paper?" Roger burst out anxiously. "I must send to Kingston too. Tom's wife's in danger Tom knows nothing of. It's my fault, but there's no time to explain it. If one of the 'prentices could take the letters to Kingston now, tonight, I'd pay my last gold piece."

138

"Would you? Then it must be a serious matter indeed. Come, I've paper and ink to spare. And Heminge's 'prentices are here—the house John's let for his family is short of beds. I'll wake Jack Rice and find a man to take him a-horseback. There are too many ruffians on the heath and the Kingston Road to send a boy alone."

Roger's shoulders had begun to feel the strain of the unaccustomed work, but the tide had turned and though the ebb had not begun to run in earnest, he kept to the deep channel where it was strongest and made fair time past Putney's church and on down the silver ribbon of water as the river slowly widened between the wooded banks and ran at last past Chelsea fields. There Roger let the current carry him for a while, and turned to look ahead where Lambeth House on the south bank grew clear against the sky and then slid slowly past. In the moonlight, the river and the town were fresh as new-minted silver, sharp-edged and true, to Roger a world both familiar and heartbreakingly new. Not even the stench from the Queen's slaughterhouse beyond Mill Bank could spoil the silvered town. The Abbey, like Lambeth House, Roger knew as well as Jack did, but Westminster Palace, the apple orchards along the bank by Lambeth Marsh, the gardens and their palaces—from Whitehall down to old Somerset House—were so lovely among their midnight trees that they seemed scarcely real.

Roger came to himself with a start of alarm to find that he had completely shipped his oars and was drifting in a slow curve down past the Strand Lane stairs. For one frightening moment he had the sense of someone or something at his back, a presence gathered like a cornered cat to pounce. There was nothing there to see, but it pulled him up sharply. Jack? Was there still Jack to fear? He might not be buried quite. . . .

Roger wavered for a moment, trying to think what to do. Tom would have headed first for the Temple, but he might be as much as an hour ahead by now, and with the Temple so near the thieves' dens of Alsatia, Roger shared the fear Jack would have had that his finery would get him robbed and killed. *Like Tony . . . set upon in the Strand.* But where would Tom go next so late? The Cardinal's Hat, where the wine was best? The lodgings in Brande's Rents? They were the most likely places. But then the name of the Blue Pump from Alan's notes leapt to his mind, and he pulled hard for the south bank and Paris Garden Stairs. The Blue Pump. "Poor Tom's Last Refuge."

There were lights behind the dingy horn-paned windows of the Windmill in Paris Garden Lane and a thin sound of revelling, but the Orange Tree was shut up with a placard on the door, and between it and the bottom of Holland Street Roger counted eight other doors sealed up. Few of the houses, stricken or no, had lit their street lamps. The sick cried out behind their walls, and somewhere beyond a curtained window a frightened child wailed thinly. Even in Holland Street where the houses were not crowded up against each other and where the gardens were dark with trees, the bright summer night was oppressive. As Roger passed one house's bridge over the drainage ditch he saw two men with a coffin frozen in the shadows under the garden fruit trees, a-sweat with fear that he might be a magistrate's man out prowling with his seals to shut them away from their livelihoods.

The bells of St. George's, St. Saviour's, and St. Olave's tolled in turn and then together for their dead.

The Castle, at the bottom of the street, was closed and dark, but at the Blue Pump, the door under the sign of a man pumping with all his might actually stood open with the thin sound of music drifting out. In the dim front room two or three determined drinkers listened to a pert old man with an untuned lute quaver out "The Ballad of Watkin's Ale" and nodded and cackled their approval.

"He's a lively old apple-john, right enough!" observed a gravelly female voice from a bench just inside the door. "And you, young sir? Are ye after lodging or only a pint of ale?"

Roger looked around the dirty, dreary little room uncomfortably. "Neither. I'm looking for someone. Garland. The player."

"Him with the King's Men? You'll not find any players here, sweet heart. They'll all have packed their precious skins off to the country. Chelmsford or Mortlake, I hear tell."

"He's come back." Roger shrank from the pudgy fingers patting at the hand he held on his purse. "If he comes here, will you tell him his brother is looking for him? I'll come back tomorrow."

"God keep ye'll be able to." The woman sighed. "I shall tell 'im, my dear, if I'm here. But look'ee—where are ye off to? There's bands of bloody ruffians abroad these nights that'll prick your gizzard for so fine a doublet as that as soon as knock'ee on the head."

"I've not far to go." Roger was vaguely uneasy at the shrewd look she gave him. She might well have her own ruffians. "I'll be back tomorrow."

"Ye're right at that, sweet heart. Trust's not for such

days as these." The woman chuckled. "God speed ye."

The house in Brande's Rents was not far, but by the time he came there and had the door locked fast behind him, Roger's heart was racing. Coming down long, straggling, tree-shadowed Maid Lane he saw that some houses in Hunt's Rents had fortified themselves against intruders by taking up their plank bridges across the deep roadside ditches. Twice where a glimmer of moonlight dipped into the dark ditch he saw bodies, the first one naked, and the second half so, with two scavengers pulling at his boot-hose and breeches while a third kept watch by their heaped-up barrow. The man's eyes had glittered at the sight of Jack's rich suit, and Roger took to his heels down toward Brande's Rents as if the devil himself were after him.

He had no key, but there was a dim light in a window downstairs where Barton the starchmaker and his family lived. After a long while a haggard Mistress Agnes came in a nightgown hastily pulled over her shift to let him in with a resentful air and a sniff of "So we're not rid of thee after all." When her own door had slammed, Roger stood in the narrow hallway to catch his breath before he climbed the steep stairs to the Garland rooms. Upstairs there was no sign anywhere that Tom had been before him. In the kitchen he found and lit a candle and saw that the cheese and the half loaf they had left that morning in the hanging bread safe—was it only so long ago as that?—had not been touched. But Tom *must* have found when he went to Cliffe's lodgings at the Temple that it had been a lie about Cliffe's baggage waiting there. He *must* come home.

Roger's stomach tightened painfully. He was on a

fool's chase, but he could not give it up. Tom would come. And when he knew what Jack had done, there would be an end to all that pain and anger and New House could sleep in peace. Roger was too tired, too full of all that he had seen, to think beyond that one, bare need: *If thou didst ever thy dear father love....*

In Jack's bedroom he stripped and sat exhausted on the bed to rub at his sore shoulders. Half in a daze, he felt himself running his hand lovingly along a leather cord around his neck and fondling a wash-leather pouch that hung from it. Puzzled, he pulled it off and opened the almost empty but oddly heavy pouch and poured out into his palm twenty-two little gold crowns.

For a moment he could only stare at the coins.

"Why you bloody little creep," he breathed at last. "He *paid* you for her!"

And he began to be afraid of Jack, waiting in the shadows of his mind.

Afraid almost to sleep. . . .

Like Iohn-a-dreames

OM DID NOT COME. IN THE MORN-
ing Roger woke with his neck and shoulders
stiff and every muscle in his body dully sore.
When he moved to turn away from the sunshine that
streamed in at the open window a pang shot across his
upper back that made him whimper aloud. For a long
moment he lay frozen in confused alarm until the long,
aching journey down the moonlit Thames from Isleworth
came back to him disjointedly, and he remembered that
he had not found Tom, nor Tom him.

The little room was somehow less familiar than it had
been by candle light. The low beamed ceiling, the high,

narrow bed with its coarse linen sheets and faded hangings, even the ewer and basin on the chest beneath the open casement window had a look of hard-edged strangeness. Roger sat up gingerly, wincing as he turned his neck, and looked round him. The Garlands' lodgings. That was where he was. Crossing to the window in his bare feet, he looked out upon a patchwork of walled gardens and tree-ringed houses, and across the lane and a deep drainage ditch, the fields and orchards of a wide park. In one field men came and went with hand-carts laden with long plank boxes and what looked like bundles of old clothes until he saw that they went among fresh-heaped graves, and tumbled the poor bundles into a wide pit. At night it would have been an eerie, frightening scene. With the sun well up and glaring on the fields, it had a flat, brightly painted unreality. The air held a threat of heat and a muggy day to come, but Roger shivered uncontrollably.

Tom's—Tom's and Katherine's—room was as oddly unfamiliar as his own, as was the pleasant little corner dining parlour that looked from its north window out across a jumble of trees and rooftops past a square, pinnacled church tower to the distant tops of a dozen spires and more. Framed in the other window was the only landmark of which he was half sure. It stood not far up the lane he had run so blindly down last night, set among the trees beyond the last of the rooftops of Brande's Rents: a large, octagonal, three-storied building, thatch-roofed and half-timbered, a vivid, sun-bright shape against a sky as blue as a painted backdrop. The Globe Theatre. Like and unlike all the pictures in the books. Roger was alarmed that it should be no more familiar than an image in a book. Last night every ditch and doorway had been familiar. But now—if the other window were looking north, as the shadows said, then the tower must be Southwark Cathedral. Beyond it would be the Thames and the church spires of the City. . . .

Roger felt frighteningly adrift. Last night he had known where he was; this morning it was as if Jack had dwindled away from his grasp, leaving him stranded in a London he did not know. Roger squeezed his eyes tightly shut, desperately trying to regain that surer footing. *The church. Southwark Cathedral was really only a copy of this one.* This was . . . St. Saviour's. And beyond were the roofs of the houses on London Bridge. The pointed tower east of the bridge on this side of the river was . . . St. Olave's! As he forced himself to see them inwardly, the names came to him. The street beyond the Globe was Maid Lane. Dead Man's Place with its stream down the middle lay a few yards to the east. Suddenly, abruptly, it was all there, as if a door he had been pushing against had been suddenly unbarred.

"It'll be all right. It has to be," Roger told himself as he went to search out something to eat. In the kitchen he found a dish of eggs, a comb of honey in a crock, and a dish of rancid butter. The eggs he broke into a bowl, and though one was bloody, they smelt all right, so he set about building a small fire in the fireplace. When it had taken hold he set the long-legged trivet over the flames, melted a knob of butter in a shallow, long-handled pan, and poured the eggs in when it had begun to sizzle. "I *will* find Tom. I will," he repeated to himself with each shake of the pan. But when he had finished eating and gone to dress himself, the food lay heavy on his stomach.

146

In the bedroom he folded Katherine's letter and tucked it for safe keeping into the pouch with the gold coins. His upper arms were still so stiff that the simple act of replacing the cord was difficult, and dressing was worse yet. The loose shirt went on easily enough, but his neck and shoulders cramped painfully as he eased on the drabbest doublet he could find: a dull mouse-coloured silk with white cutwork bands and silver buttons. The sleeves had to be laced into the doublet with silver-tagged laces first, the doublet's long row of front buttons buttoned, and the matching paned trunk hose laced through eyelets to the doublet's waist. It was a complicated job and he fumbled more than once, losing time he could ill afford to spare, but it was done at last and he hastily tied on the cork-soled shoes Jack had worn the day before.

In the parlour Roger searched out pen and paper and ink. Though his hand dragged, as if he shaped the words against its will, in the end he managed to write: *Dear Tom, Katherine was safe at Purfets' all along. It was not her. I will explain. Stay here if you come. I have gone to look for you, but will return. Jack.* Folding the note he wrote *Tom* across the face and propped it against a candlestick on the dining table. Then, on impulse, he scrawled another: *It was not K. I must see you. Brande's Rents or the Blue Pump. Jack.* He addressed it to *Tom Garland of the King's Men* and put it in the purse at his belt. He would leave it at the Cardinal's Hat. Returning to the kitchen, he lowered the food safe to cut himself enough bread and cheese for lunch, wrapping it in a piece of paper and a handkerchief and putting it into a Spanish leather pouch that had hung in Jack's wardrobe. It was already mid-morning, and the sound of carts rumbling up

147

St. Margaret's Hill and the distant cries of street-sellers in Long Southwark bid him hurry. With the waking sense of strangeness past, it was almost as if the part of him that was at home here ached to be abroad and searching too.

Roger was out and on the doorstep, looking for the key he had found and put in the shoulder-pouch, when he discovered the first note for Tom, folded small and tucked beneath the food parcel. Unfolding it in dismay, he shivered with a sudden chill and then went slowly up to prop it once more against the candlestick. *Be careful,* caution whispered. *Take care....*

Once into Dead Man's Place, Roger decided to walk to the Temple and save the waterman's two pennies. He had too little money left and would not, could not, touch the gold. Past St. Saviour's, London Bridge was strangely quiet. On an ordinary day the press was so great that anyone with the tuppence to spare could cross by water in a quarter of the time, but now the grinning heads on their pikes loured down from the entrance tower onto the thin traffic as if to cry "Abandon hope!" A grisly welcome to a deathly town.

The narrow arcades and passages between the tall houses lining the bridge were not deserted, but people hurried on their errands, hollow-eyed and harried. More than half the lamps in the dim arcades were dark, and beggars whined in shadowed doorways. Half or more of the shops were locked and shuttered, and not a few of the ornate doors to the upper stories of the houses were marked and sealed. Even so, here and there a haberdasher's boy called out, "See here, young sir, silk roses for your shoes," or "Would ye go wi'out a hat, young sir? Come see, we've French hats, hats from Florence, hats

. . ." but Roger hurried unheeding through each arcade, half dazzled by the sunny passages between where the arches opened onto the narrower, uncovered stretches of bridge. Great Nonsuch House, splendid beyond belief, he passed through and scarcely saw.

At the north end of the bridge Roger turned from the cobbled way into a side street half by dead reckoning and half remembering, aiming westward toward the Fleet and Temple Bar. The day had begun to burn in earnest, and the mingled aromas from the stockfishmongers' and the cookshops and the stench from doorside garbage heaps were overpowering. Roger was giddily unsure whether the shimmer of heat that rippled in the narrow strip of sunshine between the overhanging house fronts was in the air or in his mind. In a deepening daze at the city's squalor and splendour, he threaded his way past coffin-carts and dunghills, on past Bridewell and the alleys of Alsatia, and came at last to the Temple.

"Why, you ha' missed him, lad," said the stout and melancholy porter when at last he answered the bell. "You ha' missed him twice, if 'tis a tall, dark, slim fellow wi' a trim beard you want, in a pepper-coloured silk lined wi' apricock."

"That's him. He would have been asking after Harry Cliffe."

"Aye he was. Last midnight, and him out with no link-boy to light him his way. I told him Mr. Cliffe and his baggage've been gone this sennight to the Earl of North-umberland at Syon. If the Earl be gone from there, says I, mayhap they've all gone north to wild Northumberland to 'scape the sickness and the heat, and would that I were with 'em! As for where in Essex young Cliffe calls home,

149

I've never heard. There's a cousin out at Bushey that has him to stay sometimes, where I've had to send his letters, but I forget the name. Now if 'twere *me*, as I said to your friend, I'd ask at the inn at Highgate. Travellers for the north must rest their beasts awhile after Highgate Hill, and the landlord won't have forgot a peacocky gallant like young Cliffe." The man snorted. "He's well enough remembered at every inn 'twixt here and the Hoop."

Highgate. And the roads to Bushey went either by way of Hampstead or Kilburn. Simple enough for a reckless and determined man to walk from Highgate to Hampstead and down to the inn at Kilburn to ask after a gallant in pale silk and a fair, blue-eyed young woman with an old Florentine-stitched cloak bag. *And to return to the Temple by way of St. John's Wood and Lillestone, Tyburn and St. Giles.* Poor Tom, bound to time's wheel by the strength of his love and hatred . . . and Tony bound with him.

"Are ye all right, lad?" The porter looked at Roger with concern, but drew back warily. " 'Tis more like August, this heat, than the tail end o' June."

"I'm all right. It's just . . ." June? Not August? But that was not important. Roger caught at the memory that had almost slipped away. "You said I'd missed him twice. When he came back had he hurt his hand?"

"Aye." The porter's look was more doubtful yet. "How d'ye know that? 'Twas but five o' the clock and no more than grey in the east when the watch came a-knockin' with their staves at my gate. They bade me keep 'im in my lodge awhile. I gave 'im a pot of ale, but no sooner had I brought to mind a nuncle young Cliffe went to in Cheapside for a meal of a Sunday than your friend was off again.

The more fool he. There's none astir at that hour but rogues and knaves, and he'd already near lost his purse to the knife that cut 'im."

"But he went anyway?"

"Aye, poor fellow. To sit upon the doorstep, I'll warrant, for the householder's a nut-pated fool who opens to a knock before day. And I would ha' been glad of his company for an hour or two. Wi' the lodgings here all but emptied and my gossips at the Rose all stowed underground but one, the days are flat as Lenten pancakes. Now that Bartholomew Fair's been forbid, there's naught to look forward to but drink and watchin' the dead go by."

Roger edged impatiently toward the gate. "Cheapside, you said?" he asked, breaking the garrulous flood of words. "That uncle of Master Cliffe's, what was his name?"

"Barentine. Ballantine? Something like. Must ye go? Aye, of course ye must." The man sighed. "Jesu keep thee."

Cheapside was not far, but twice Roger lost his way and stumbled through dark, unpaved lanes the sun had not pried into. When he came out at last onto the broad, clean, tree-shaded street and saw, past Bread Street, the block of splendid houses that outdid all their prosperous neighbours, he felt more than ever as if he walked in an unreal world. Four storeys tall, ornate, with handsome timbering, glittering with wide expanses of windows, each house with gilded rainspouts and the carved and gilt Goldsmiths' arms—in that brilliant, heavy air they shimmered like the shifting images of dreams.

Ballantine. Barentine. He must ask in one of the shops.

151

Those along the splendid row were goldsmiths' and most were shuttered tight, but in one a gold candelabrum was displayed against a black brocade in the shop window, and the upstairs casements were open wide. Roger's knocking brought a polite assistant to point out Barentines' and say that they had gone away three days before in two hired coaches, no telling where.

Sore and tired and frightened, Roger sat under a sycamore tree to cut his cheese and bread for a sandwich. The bread was stale, the cheese strong, and together they made him fiercely thirsty. His headache had returned with the deepening of the heavy, humid heat, and he felt too hopelessly confused and muddled to know what he should do. If he had something to drink . . . but what was safe that would not make his muddle even worse? Small-beer. Near-beer. Schoolboys drank small-beer. Roger giggled, half in panic, at remembering that. He had read it in a schoolbook three hundred and seventy-odd years from now. But then he sobered, chilled despite the heat. "That's a queer thought," he said aloud. "I must be dizzied from the sun." He should have ha'pennies enough for half a barrel of small-beer. He must find the nearest tavern. Then he could think what to do next.

Fumbling in the purse at his belt, Roger's fingers touched a folded paper among the coins, and in dismay he drew out the note he had meant to leave at the Cardinal's Hat. Two silver three-farthing pieces dropped from a second folded paper and rolled away unheeded as Roger stared at the tightly folded note. Surely he had brought and forgotten only—written only—the one? But even as he unfolded the second paper he knew that it was not a copy. It was the other note, the longer one beginning

Katherine was safe at Purfets' all along. He had climbed the stairs to prop it a second time against the candlestick, *had* propped it there, and still had brought it way with him. *"He"? No, Jack.*

He would have to go back. If Tom—*when* Tom fell ill, it was to Brande's Rents he would go. He might be there now, and ill. *When Tom fell ill*. . . . Roger stiffly pushed himself erect, but it was Jack's panic that sent him headlong down the narrow, crooked lanes to Blackfriars Stairs where he hailed a waterman and paid four of his ha'-pennies to cross to the water stairs at the top of Thames Street. The white-painted walls of the old stews and taverns along Bankside glittered across the river, and Roger kept his eyes fast on the red sign of the Cardinal's Hat all through the crossing as if he could will Tom to be there. The Cardinal's Hat . . . why did it stick in his mind? The note, that was it. He must ask there for news of Tom and leave his note.

No one had seen Tom Garland at the Cardinal's Hat, where the clock in the front room chimed half-past five as Roger came through the door. Could it be so late? Had he slept under that sycamore tree? How could it be so late and still no Tom?

The landlord propped the note atop a wine cask and drew Roger's small-beer himself. "Now away wi' ye and drink it out of doors," he growled. "I may be a friend to Tom Garland but I'll not have ye sickening under my roof."

" 'Tis only the heat. I'm not ill." Only the hellish heat. But there was no point in arguing. He took his pint out and along Bankside to the shade of a tree hanging over the garden wall of one of the Pike Garden houses, where he could catch his breath. "Jack, my lad," he said thickly, "if Tom has caught his death 'tis all your doing. He cannot stay in town. Must come away. So stir yourself, you addlepated cuckoo."

Somewhere deep in his mind the dim alarm sounded. *Not Jack. Roger. You're Roger.*

Jack pushed himself unsteadily erect. "It doesn't really matter," he whispered. "Only Tom matters."

Tom came sore-footed home at nightfall to Brande's Rents to find the door sealed up and the quarantine order nailed upon the doorpost. His knock on the window by the door fetched first a snively child and then poor Agnes Barton to say it was her James and the youngest of the children who were ill. There was nothing yet that they needed, so Tom had wished her a peaceful night for James and was almost as far as the playhouse when Agnes suddenly remembered Jack and came back to her window to call down the lane. To Tom's alarm that Jack should be in town at all, and looking ill at that, all she could say was, "The poor lad said, 'Tell Tom the Blue Pump.' Nothing but that, over and over. 'Tell Tom the Blue Pump.' "

And Jack was there. Rough-voiced old Alison Yarbie, the hostess, had against all reason taken him in, untrussed his laces, stripped him down to his linen shirt, and put him in a clean bed. "Such a pretty lad to leave to the cutthroats or the ditch," she said, puffing up the stairs ahead of Tom with the candlestick. "Let 'em seal up my door if they will. I had my touch o' the sickness in April, and I've drink and flour for forty days, with hens and cabbages and cowcumbers in my garden *And* a little door out into the fields and away."

Hours later pain woke Jack from darkness and a shapeless dream into a guttering circle of light, the chill of a cold cloth on his burning forehead, and a thin runnel of water past his ear and down his neck. On a bench near the bed a single candle burned in a pewter candlestick beside a basin filled with water. Tom sat on a joint-stool drawn close to the bed, round-shouldered with exhaustion, his face streaked with tears and the day's grime. He wrung out a rag over the basin to fold and smooth across Jack's forehead.

"Oh, Jack." He groaned. "I thought you well away to Brentford with young Somercote. *Why* must you have followed me back into this pesthole?" Covering his face with his hands, he said brokenly, " 'Tis hard enough my Kitten should leave me for a tinsel gallant. Now you have caught your death and I must lose you both."

to say we end The hart-ake

THRUST OUT OF TIME INTO A WORLD of shadow, Roger huddled on a bench in a corner of the dark room and watched the boy on the bed. Outside, beyond the open, unshuttered windows, the sun beat cheerfully down on streets and marshy fields, but the room was strangely dark, a room seen in a dark mirror. He had cut himself adrift from Jack . . . a day ago? Two days? The illness had frightened him at last into letting go his increasingly fragile hold. What was the use of it all anyway? Jack had fought too fiercely against mending what he had broken. He would never say a word of Katherine. Roger knew that now. Jack's anxiety for Tom's safety had lasted only so long as he did not understand his own danger. When the telltale swellings betrayed his weary heaviness and raging thirst for what they were, he clung to Tom as he clung to life. No matter that the love keeping Tom by him could mean Tom's death as well. No matter that the tale of what he had done might be pieced together if Tom lived. But why should Tom live? Roger's interference had changed nothing else. How could it change that? It had, it seemed, done nothing but trap him in a nightmare. In that bare, low-ceilinged room he was a poor, trapped shadow no one saw but Jack.

Tom slept when he could, as now, on the truckle-bed pulled over to the open window. Jack slept only fitfully and had bad dreams. Each time he wakened, his feverish eyes wandered anxiously until they fixed on Roger, as if to fix where danger lay.

Tell him! Haven't you hurt him enough?

I'm afraid. He'll leave me if he knows. I'm afraid . . .

He'll piece it together for himself, you know. In time.

A queer kind of satisfaction grew in those sick eyes. *He'll never. He'll go with me. He's sickening himself and feels in his dreams for swellings.*

No!

But Tom in his uneasy sleep did lie cramped upon his side, arms crossed, his hands pressed tightly into his armpits.

There was a quiet tap at the door and Mistress Yarbie bustled in, still puffing from the stairs, to set a pitcher on the bench beside the bed and take away the emptied one. Tom jerked awake when she passed between Jack's bed and his, and she gave him a pitying look as he sat up on the low truckle-bed, head in his hands. "You've a touch of it yourself, my lad, by the look of ye. I'll be setting the Pump up for a pest-house next. Old Timkins up in the garret's sickening fast, and I'm a fool as ever was, running up and down. Handsome and young or too old to kick up a dust, I'm a fool for any of ye." She mopped at her face with a grimy handkerchief.

Tom's grin as he stood was wan. "A dear old fool, then. How—how's Jack, d'you think?"

The old woman shook her head doubtfully. "It came on him so fast. Else he was sickening before and wouldn't give in to it. 'Twould make it worse. He's been thrashin' in his sleep, by the look of the bed linen. I brought another nice lemon and borage julep to ease the thirst when he wakes. There's sorrel water in it for the fever." She hesitated. "If ye'd like a chicken again for your dinner I'll send out to the cookshop, but I'll need the silver for't and for what I've laid out already. 'Tis three shillings for the lemons and oranges and eight shillings tuppence for the chickens and mutton and th' giblet pie."

Tom flushed as he opened his purse. "I had forgot. I tipped tavernkeepers and ostlers from Gyl's to Highgate and Stratford East for news of—of an old acquaintance, so that after the physician yesterday and his pills, I've only the eight and tuppence. If you've an honest messenger, I can send for more to Mortlake tomorrow."

Old Alison shrugged. "If you wish. But the lad has coin enough and to spare."

Tom looked wryly up from counting his coins. "Jack? Hardly. Unless it's farthings enough to make a deceitful pretty jingle."

"No indeed," Mistress Yarbie insisted. " 'Tis gold, and

plenty. In a pouch beneath his shirt. I felt how heavy 'twas when I undid his doublet." At a sound from the bed she gave a sudden start. "Heaven 'fend us, the poor child's demon-shot for sure!"

For Jack had wrenched about in terror. *No, no gold!* he wanted to cry out, but his swollen tongue muffled it to a violent "Oh, oh!"

"Bless us, what is't he stares at so?" the old woman whispered, so far forgetting herself as to sketch a rapid sign of the cross on her ample bosom. "He stares in that corner as if 'twere a bogle come to fetch him."

"It's all right, Jack lad," Tom soothed. "I'm here. I'm here." He raised his brother up to ease his retching cough, but as he lowered him again to the pillows he felt a thickness shift between Jack's shoulder blades, and traced through the damp linen the cord it hung by. Jack struggled weakly, but the pouch came free and Tom gently drew the knotted cord over his head and smoothed the damp hair away from the boy's flushed face.

"It feels heavy as gold, right enough," Tom muttered. "I saw the cord before and thought it only some pretty friendship knot. But gold? When he spends the shillings I give him each week in a day or three and begs for more?" He spilled the pouch out on the truckle-bed.

"Lord ha' mercy!" old Alison whispered. "How much is't?"

"Four—*five* pounds and more," Tom said uneasily. "Jack?"

Jack made no sign that he had heard, but mumbled violently in his fever, glaring into the corner of the room with such despairing fury that Alison Yarbie, with a fearful glance over her shoulder, moved her stout self to stand between the corner and the boy. Only then did Jack's eyes stray toward Tom's back as he unfolded the papers from the pouch and read slowly, uncomprehendingly, the greeting *My onely dere swete hart. . . .*

When Tom came to the end of the third sheet he looked up dazedly. "What can it mean? 'Tis my wife's hand. She looks for me to come quick as I may, yet. . . . How came Jack by these? When was it writ? And she's not signed it. It seems scarce finished." He read through it once more in disbelief and wakening alarm.

"The letter Kitten left at New House. . . . It bore no greeting," Tom whispered, turning at last. "And this one no farewell. They belong together. They belong together, Jack." He looked at his brother helplessly. *"What have you done to me?"*

Roger heard Tom's words cleave through the deepening shadows and hang in the room's heavy heat like the unbelieving cry of some dumb animal struck down by his master's hand. Even before Mistress Yarbie moved aside, he knew Jack would make no answer. Jack's eyes were fixed on him in fear and hatred and did not see the old woman take his purse from the peg on the wall where his clothes hung and draw out the note that, but for Jack, would still have leaned against the candlestick in the empty rooms in Brande's Rents. "What o' this?" she asked, thrusting it at Tom. "I saw before 'twas for thee and forgot it."

Roger could not see Tom's face, but it hardly mattered. Tom would guess the rest. It was finished. By chance almost, but finished. For Roger, if not for the Garlands.

I'm afraid. Despair whispered in the shadows. *Tom. . . .*

He won't leave you. Roger tried to pierce that be-wildered pain. *He loves you. And you don't even know what that means. You. . . .*

The words died into silence like sparks falling into dark water. There was no Jack, no room, nothing but the streaming darkness.

what may this meane?...?

OGER WONDERED IDLY IF HE WERE
drowning. He could not move to save himself
and could not seem to care. In a darkness where
there was no sound, only a faint rise and fall of lulling
motion, a sense of floating in emptiness, nothing seemed to
matter. Not to care—that was the answer. Why struggle to
tie up on this bank or that when it was the way of mooring lines to fray and break and send one adrift over deeper
and deeper waters? Easier far to drift. . . .

But something held him back: a hail from an unseen
shore, a hand on a trailing line. For a long time while he
swung against that line, until weariness and confusion

ebbed and the darkness thinned. The lulling warmth bled away and he felt cold, and wet.

Roger!

Roger stirred and felt a tugging at his hand.

Roger? Oh, Rog, please be all right.

A second small hand closed around his own. Pippa? How could Pippa have come to the edge of nowhere? With an effort that left him drained of everything but wonder, Roger opened his eyes to stare up at her in bewilderment.

"Are you O.K.?" Pippa's voice quavered. "Oh Rog, I was so scared you'd slip clear in. What happened? Is he gone?"

Pippa, in her dressing gown and pyjamas, barefooted and shivering, crouched above him on the slipway, clinging to his hand for dear life. Fog drifted around them, moon-pale, and dark shapes loomed above.

"A dream," Roger said, the words coming thickly and slowly. "I went to help Tom so Pa'd be free of him and almost lost myself."

"Roger, *please*," Pippa pleaded.

"It's all right. I'm all right."

But when he rolled onto his side and drew his feet up under him, he found not his camp bed, but a hard, slanted surface and the slap and pull of water. That much had been no dream. Startled into wakefulness at last, he sat up and saw that he really *was* on the slipway, shirtless and cold, with his legs half in the river. The dark shapes above were parked cars, dimly haloed by the street lamps across the way.

"One of your sandals floated away," Pippa said. "I didn't see the other one. Can you stand up? The fog's getting thinner. We ought to go before anybody sees us."

Roger tried to make out the hands on his watch and could not. He scrambled up, his jeans slapping coldly at his calves. "What time is it?"

"Almost morning, I think. But Mama and Alan still weren't back from the hospital when you came out." Pippa took Roger's hand and drew him after her like an obedient child up to the parking area, across the street, and along the footpath past the church, where the old-fashioned street lamps marked their way like pale candles in the fog.

Beyond the river the fog thinned quickly and they had almost reached their own lane when Pippa ventured again to ask, "Roger? What *did* happen?"

"I don't know," Roger said helplessly. "Not for sure. How did you know I was out here?"

Pippa slowed and peered questioningly upward, but Roger's face was in shadow, silhouetted against the chill glare of a Park Road arc-lamp. "It *wasn't* a dream, you know. I saw him. That Jack. I saw him when you were trying to get the letters out of his hidey-hole."

Roger looked down at her wonderingly. She stood at the road's edge in her bare feet as matter-of-factly as if she made a nightly habit of strange expeditions. "And you followed. Just like that?" He broke off as a car's head-lamps winked into sight far up Park Road and pulled Pippa after him at a run the last few yards to the lane. Once safe in its shadows they picked their way along gingerly.

"It's a good thing it's so grassy," Pippa said, thinking of her bare feet. "I ran like sixty and couldn't catch up to him—to you, I mean. And then I was scared somebody'd be awake on Church Street and look out a window, so I went along between the fence and the parked cars or I mightn't have found you. You weren't down there at first, before the fog. I don't know *where* you were. And when the fog came, it came so sneaky-fast that everything but the slipway just disappeared. One minute you weren't anywhere, and then you were down there looking like you'd gone to sleep. I couldn't wake you up or pull you out. I was afraid if I went for help you'd slip on in. Besides, it felt—spooky. So I just hung on."

Roger shivered. "I probably wouldn't be here if you hadn't. Was it really only as long as that? It seemed like . . . like three days. And wasted ones, at that." There was no time to tell it all. It had seemed so simple and was not. At Pippa's nod he said miserably, "All that about 'being an actor in the past'? I fancied myself putting everything right for everybody. It sounded so simple. But it didn't work that way. Oh, I think that what I did warned Katherine and let Tom know the truth about Jack's trick, so we won't have our ghost any more, but I have an idea it didn't change anything that *happened*. Maybe that's just from not *knowing* what happened, but. . . ." The sense of powerlessness dragged at him. He had liked Tom. Loved him, even. And not to know was unbearable.

"Oh Pips," he whispered. "He was so much like Pa."

"Well," Pippa said kindly, tucking her hand in his, "we'll just have to find out what did happen. Like Alan and Jo found out about him in the first place."

"Alan—" Roger stopped abruptly where the drive curved to approach the house. "Alan's car's still gone," he said tightly. "They're not back. What if—Oh, Pips, maybe I should have gone with Pa in the first place!

Come on. I'm going to put on some shoes and a shirt and walk round to the hospital. You can tell Jemmy if she wakes up."

"Wait," Pippa hissed. She felt in her pocket for the key. "It's locked. Jemmy was asleep and all alone, so I locked it."

"It's not locked now." Roger eased the door open quietly and moved quickly towards the hall stairs.

"Roger!" Pippa's quaver caught him on the landing.

"What is it?" he whispered. "And keep it down. You'll wake Jemmy."

Pippa did not answer. In the faint light from the window in the lower hall he saw her point at something in the front room and then disappear. Forgetting Jemmy, he took the steps noisily two at a time and, reaching the doorway, groped for the light switch.

The light did not come on. And the moon-like paper globe was gone from the shadowed ceiling.

"Pippa? What is it? What's the matter?"

Pippa closed the door at the far end of the room and moved into a patch of moonlight. "Jemmy's not there," she said wonderingly. "The *bed*'s gone too. And look!"

This time Roger saw what she pointed at. The doorway up into the dining room was incredibly, nonsensically, covered up again. Instead of the plain stone arch and patches of dark brick wall there was a heavy, painted moulding topped with a cumbersome lintel crenellated like a castle's parapet. In the dining room itself, the old gas stove huddled in its dark hole in a fireplace wall with ruined panelling. Opposite, beside the door to the kitchen stairway, was a wall of peeling cupboard doors.

The beautiful Elizabethan fireplace and the wide, handsome staircase were gone, erased, as if they had never been.

8 I will finde
Where truth is hid

THEN ROGER WOKE ALL OF HIS WIN-
dows were wide open and through the one
looking out over the green garage roof the sun
rising above Syon Park glittered through the trees. It
was the first morning in Isleworth all over again, an
astonishing, unexpected stitching-up of the rent in time:
poor Tom's ghost would never walk. Had no call to.

Roger could not grasp it at first, it was at once so simple and so beyond explaining. That Tom's ghost would
not appear again he had guessed, but not that his own
interference in the past would have changed the present.
And, of course, it had to. Once Tom Garland knew that

167

he had not lost Katherine, it made no difference whether he died in the plague or in his happy old age: his ghost would not walk for grief of her. And that meant that these five days past when he *had* walked would have to be either impossibly full of gaps, or ... gone. Undone. To be re-done as he had re-done Jack's last three days.

From the window overlooking the back garden came the aroma of bacon frying. For a long, blank moment Roger could not think what to do, what it would mean to have those five days back, and then—to his surprise—he knew he did not mean to worry about it. He scrambled out of the sleeping bag so eagerly that the low camp bed tipped over on its side and gave him a sharp crack on the elbow. He hardly noticed, but headed, shivering, for the rear window. The long shadow of the house lay across the tangled back garden, but below, at the corner by the kitchen areaway, Bast lay stretched on his back in the one shaft of sunlight. Beyond, down along the garden wall, Roger caught a glimpse of his father's dark head moving along a shaggy row of box trees and felt a great contentment. Directly below and to the right, on the patch of terrace at the foot of the French-door steps, Jo had set up the camp stove and was turning bacon in the frying pan with as much easy elegance of gesture as if she were conducting Mozart instead of breakfast. It was eerie—seeing the day begin just as it had the first time through.

But it was too chilly still to stand watching. Roger rooted in his rucksack and brought out the same riotously bright T-shirt. Jemmy had presented it to him because Alan refused to be seen in it. On an empty stomach it did look alarmingly violent, and it wasn't really warm enough, so—feeling like an echo of himself

—he pulled his old green cotton polo-neck on over it and hurried down the upstairs hall.

Breakfast was spread higgledy-piggledy on the door-table in the dining-room and Pippa sat in the doorway to the garden, wiping clean her eggy plate with a piece of toast. As she turned, Roger had a moment of panic. If Pippa didn't remember.... And then he met her nervous, questioning look and knew that she had felt that same brief flicker of doubt.

"I haven't said a word," she whispered owlishly. "It's *weird*."

"Not weird, weirdly wonderful!" Roger declared with a flourish of the milk jug.

Jo peered indoors from her post at the stove. "'Hark! there's one up!' Roger, and at eight o'clock? Wonder of wonders!"

Roger struck a pose in the doorway. "'The busy day, waked by the lark, hath roused the ribald crow.'"

"And fielding Shakespeare at that! You'll have bacon, won't you?"

"Yes, please." Roger cut three slices of bread and clattered down the iron steps past Pippa. "Is there room for this much toast?"

Jo moved over. "For you, always. But you'd better fetch a fork if you don't want to burn yourself turning it. I take it you slept well?"

"Like the proverbial." Roger bounded back up the steps as Pippa moved to let him by. He came back, fork in hand, to hesitate in the doorway. "On second thought, that's not precisely true."

Pippa set her plate behind her. "We went down to the river in the middle of the night," she announced baldly.

169

"It was high tide. Roger fell in and I had to hang on until he could climb out."

"You *what*?" Jo turned to stare at them in astonishment.

Roger flushed. "Not right in. Only on the slipway." Trust Pippa to plunge straight in.

"But what on earth were you—" Jo broke off as Tony appeared along the north-west fence and came, plate in hand, picking his way through the brambles. "Tony, these two were down messing about in the Thames in the middle of the night."

Tony gave Roger a sharp look. "Might one inquire why?" he drawled.

"I suppose," Roger said carefully, "one might say one was out exorcising the household ghost."

"I wasn't aware that we had one," said Jo with a glimmer of amusement. But there was an odd, guarded interest, too, in the look she gave him.

"We *did* have," Pippa declared.

Tony recovered quickly from the moment's mood that had frozen him, frowning, at the terrace-edge and came to peer at the bacon. "I'm disappointed in you, Rog," he said lightly. "A little night breeze moans through that colander of a ceiling and you begin coining ghosts. Not that we're not well-placed for it. I see we're smack up against the churchyard on that side." He nodded in the direction of the river with a ghoulish waggle of eyebrows as he speared a half-toasted slice of bread with his fork and held it out to Jo on his plate. "None of your brittle, dried-up rashers, now. The three fatty ones will do nicely."

Roger, bemused, watched the unfinished toast, wrapped

round the bacon, disappear. Everything was both the same and different. It was strange to think that the better part of a week had ceased to exist; that Tony would never play Tom Garland playing Hamlet; that Tom would never carry him into the shadows of that "undiscovered country" from which there is no returning. Roger found himself thinking—wonderingly, for it was quite un-Rogerly—that if he acted at risk, half blindly, on what he knew and felt in that strange past time, with no knowing what he might have set in motion, the same really should go here and now. Last night Pippa had not muddled around looking for reassuring explanations and slippers, but had run after him barefooted into the dark. Tony and Jo too.... Their feelings braided them together and to others like strands of music improvised upon the moment, unstrained and sure. Oh, in a bad temper they snapped. When they disagreed, they went at it hammer and tongs. But their laughter was infectious, and they spent it with pleasure.

Improvisation. The actor and musician knew improvisation as a discipline of art. Perhaps—perhaps that same spontaneity of response was a discipline of life, and lives he had thought formless held a shifting harmony he had not suspected. That was Jo and Tony's security. No warm nest. No guarantee of the day after tomorrow. It was as simple as knowing who or what you cared for and acting on it. Jack, now: perhaps Jack had *felt* love for Tom, but the real love, the love he *acted*, was for himself. Perhaps in that one thing, thought Roger, he and Jack had been brothers. Love unacted was not love.

"Rog? Your toast needs turning."

Roger looked up to find Jo watching him curiously

and flushed as he forked the bread over.

"A penny for 'em," Jo teased.

"No charge." Roger tended to arranging the toast with unnecessary care. "I was wondering whether it was you I love or the crispy way you do bacon. At a pinch I think I could do without the bacon."

Jo laughed. "You did get out on the right side of the bed this morning! Tell you what. I'll put on three more pieces so that you'll be in no danger of running short on either." She cast him an odd, sideways look. "*If* you'll tell us this ghost story of yours."

Roger looked across at his father speculatively. "I might, if Pa would promise to keep quiet until the end."

Tony looked wounded to the bone. "Oh, come now! Would I laugh?" Hand on his heart, he turned to look at the ungainly, ugly house. "Actually, I suppose I might. I can't think when I've seen a house with less spirit. I refuse to believe that anything so kitschy could be distinguished by a ghost." The offhanded tone could not conceal a gleam of wary interest.

"But I *saw* one of them," Pippa insisted passionately. "He had dark, curly hair with longer curls down in front of his ears, and a wine-y-coloured suit."

Tony seemed a bit nonplused at such vehemence from commonsensical Pippa. "Oh, well then," he said gamely, going to sit on the iron steps, "I suppose I must promise to hold my tongue."

Jo, when they had heard the tale, stood speechless for a moment and then turned her attention to the bacon, stabbing jerkily at the burned rashers to push them away from the coals. "That's quite a story! It sounds. . . ." But then she did not say what it sounded like.

Tony's reaction was the surprising one. His interest had changed by uneasy degrees to a deep disquiet as he watched and listened more and more intently. "An oddly circumstantial bit of moonshine," he said at last. "You do surprise me, young Nicholas. Where'd you ever hear of Tom Garland?"

"There actually *was* such a person?" asked Jo.

Tony hesitated. He looked puzzled, half alarmed. "The name's certainly—familiar. I suppose I could've read somewhere that a Thomas Garland was Shakespeare's first Guildenstern. The queer thing is...." The words came slowly, reluctantly. "It's more like a thing remembered than a dry fact met in a book. As if—but it *had* to be a dream. It's sheer nonsense to say that five days can slip out from under one's feet as if time could ebb as well as flow. And yet the whole tale sounds so bloody familiar! Or bits and snatches of it do. Idiotic things like Alan and Jemmy's having been here and our uncovering the Elizabethan house. Most of it's a muddle, though. And how ... *how* could I remember being Tom and filling in for Burbage as Hamlet?"

"I don't be*lieve* all this. But there was a *Guardian* review," Jo said dazedly. "I remember cutting it out. I meant to have it framed. There was one bit—" Closing her eyes, she quoted hesitantly, " '*I left the theatre ... with the impression that ... I had been holding my breath for three and three-quarters hours. What Tony Nicholas gave us last night may not have been Hamlet as Burbage played him under Shakespeare's direction, but it is a* Hamlet *that brushes away three and three-quarters centuries to make the past—*' "

173

"'—our *vivid present,*'" Tony finished for her. "A review like that.... Dream or no, it gives me an itch to stir things up, come Monday night." He grinned shakily.

"How could it have been a dream?" Pippa objected. "Four people don't dream up the same story, not and have all the bits fit."

"Neither, in the general way of things, do they get two runs at the same week," Tony said wryly. "But why quibble? Alan's due down tomorrow, and we can put him onto this Tom Garland. He loves a riddle. And if there was such a person, he's bound to turn him up at the Senate House library or on a top shelf at the Drama League."

"You can look him up in the old parish registers *today* if you don't believe it all happened," Roger said passionately.

"Or," offered Pippa, finishing off the last of her third piece of toast and delicately licking the jam from her fingers, "you could look under the rotten floorboards up in Roger's room."

The tale in the telling had seemed to Roger no less vivid than the five lost days had been in the living of them, but already, disconcertingly, it had begun to take on the distant vividness of story or dream, as it had for Jo and Tony. When he found his palms sweating on the tire iron as he and Tony ripped up the rotten flooring, Roger wondered whether there might not come a time when he doubted the tale himself. For it was true and not-true. Just as those three days so long ago had been re-done, the five just past would be. Two separate realities now and in the past. But surely the *house* was the same....

174

It did not take long. Through a hole ripped open in a matter of minutes, the beam from Jo's flashlight picked out the broad, dust-thick stairs and, in a dusty cobwebbed jumble on the landing, the dismantled upper railings, newel post, and balusters.

They ripped the hole as wide as could be managed without a proper wrecking-bar, and Roger lowered himself awkwardly into the cramped space below. In Tony's and Jo's dumb-struck silence he moved down the dust-soft treads to the landing and with his hands brushed off the great round knob of the landing newel post. Wrapping both arms round it, he strained forward and back to work the knob loose, circling round the post as he did so. It was awkward work. He had to keep hunched over because of the flooring inches above his head.

"Like a dirty great champagne cork," Tony observed nervously. He sat on the top step with Pippa on his lap and an arm round Jo, who shivered with excitement.

And then it came free.

Roger thrust one grimy hand into the cavity. When he drew it out, his eyes were shining.

Almost as brightly as the gold coins that glittered in his palm.

Had I but time...
ô I could tell you

EPILOGUE

WHEN ALAN COLLET WENT ON Monday to the Senate House library, he went with the eerie sense that each step, each gesture made, each page he turned was an echo of motions already made, of pages already scanned. Even the notes he made in the little notebook were the same—all but the last. A footnote reference to the parish church attended by actors from the Globe sent him to an obscure little history book, and then to the church itself. These last notes read:

Memorial plaque in St. Saviour's recorded in W. M. Goss,
   The history and antiquities of the parish Church

176

of St. Saviour, Southwark (1819). Seems to have
been lost in the demolition and rebuilding of 1838–
41. Plaque read:

IOHN GARLAND OF THIS PARISH ·
DEPARTED THIS LIFE IULY THE
1^S · 1603 BEING AGED 14
YEARES 7 MONTHES AND 9 DAYES ·
HE LYETH IN WYNCHESTRE FIELDE

Confirmed by St. Saviour's register of burials.
Entry for 2 July 1603 reads:

> *Iohn Garlan, apprentice, buried with*
> *a forenoone knell of the great bell,*
> *xx s.*

Roger and Jo, poring together over pages of crabbed
handwriting in records as far afield as Kingston and
Mortlake pieced together only the barest bones of Tom
Garland's mended life, but those few were enough to tell
more of a tale than they looked to find.

From the parish register of christenings, Church of St. Mary
the Virgin, Mortlake:

24 September [1603]	*Christopher, son of Thomas Garland, player, and Katherine his wife.*
The same Daye	*Also Susan, davghter of the said Thomas and Katherine.*

From the parish register of burials, All Saints' Church,
Isleworth:

26 December 1603	*Buried in the church with a knell of III for the monthes of his lyf, Christopher, infant*

177

son of Thomas Garland,
pl.. .r and Katherine, of New
Howse . . . . . . .rsonidge.

3 May 1642	*Buried this day, Katherine, wife to Thomas Garland of this parish, in the churchyard.*
9 May 1642	*This day was buried in the churchyard Thomas Garland of New House, vestryman of this Church.*

From the register of marriages, All Saints' Church, Isleworth:

21 June 1621	*Susan, daughter of Thomas Garland of New House to Gilbert Cox, farmer of this parish.*

The tale had come full circle.